W9-BPL-120

TIME

TIME

A Jason Caldwell Mystery

ROGER REID

Junebug Books

Montgomery | Louisville

Junebug Books
105 South Court Street
Montgomery, AL 36104

Published in the United States by Junebug Books,
a division of NewSouth, Inc., Montgomery, Alabama.

Library of Congress Cataloging-in-Publication Data

Reid, Roger.
Time / Roger Reid.
p. cm.
Sequel to: Space.
Summary: Searching for fossils at the Steven C. Minkin Paleozoic
Footprint Site, near Birmingham, Alabama, fourteen-year-old Jason
and his friend Leah uncover a fossil thief and find an old enemy
hunting them.

ISBN-13: 978-1-58838-262-7
ISBN-10: 1-58838-262-1

[1. Fossils—Fiction. 2. Paleontology—Fiction. 3. Criminals—Fiction.
4. Alabama—Fiction.] I. Title.
PZ7.R27333Ti 2010
[Fic]—dc22

2010025671

Design by Randall Williams
Printed in the United States of America

Learn more about *Time* at
www.newsouthbooks.com/time
www.rogerreidbooks.com

FOR EMILY

CONTENTS

1

TICK

It was 4:10. Then it was 4:45. And there was nothing in between.

Then it was five minutes after five.

At twenty minutes till six, I was able to see beyond the watch hanging from my belt, and I could see that my feet were pointed uphill. I remember thinking, *I've rolled down a mountain before.*

Then it was six o'clock.

No pain, I said to myself, and I think I said it out loud.

I tried to sit up. I rose up on my elbows. It was too steep. I didn't want to lie back down, so I scooted around to get my feet lower than my head. The rocks beneath me wobbled with an odd sound. *Horses*—it sounded like horses clomping down a city street.

Then it was 6:15.

I know because I glanced at my watch when I sat up to look down. It was about fifty yards to the bottom of the steep slope where I was resting. *Fifty yards, that would be about forty-five meters*, I thought. I was trying to get my brain working. I twisted around to look back over my shoulder. I could see up about one hundred yards to where the gray rocks seemed to disappear into a gray sky. *One hundred yards would be about ninety meters.*

Who cares?

And then it was 6:35.

I was surrounded by gray. Gray rocks. A gray sky. There was even a gray smell. That smell, I realized, was me. My shirt was soaked with sweat. *I need a shower,* I said, and this time I know I said it out loud.

I sat up and rested my hands on my knees. I bent at the waist and let my head drop down which shifted my weight just enough to cause me to slide downhill a few feet. I leaned back and caught myself. The sound of horses on pavement rattled around me as the rocks wobbled. There was no other sound. There were no songbirds singing. There were no crows cackling. No wind. And no voices. There should be voices. Someone calling to me. Someone shouting to see if I was hurt.

Maybe they couldn't see me.

Leah! I shouted. *Leah, I'm down here!*

I don't remember lying back down. I don't remember closing my eyes. I don't remember opening my eyes. I just remember being on my back and staring into a gray sky. The sky was close, like if I could stand, I could reach up and touch it. I sat up, tried to stand, flipped over, and rolled several feet down the slope.

This time there was pain. Most of the pain was in my knees and elbows. *Pain can be a good thing,* I thought. *It lets you know you're still alive.*

I eased myself up on my aching elbows and looked down between my feet. The last time I rolled down a mountain a tree broke my fall. I looked down the steep slope. There was nothing between me and the fall to the bottom.

I glanced at my watch. It was 6:54—*a.m. or p.m.*, I wondered. It had to be p.m. If it were the morning, it would have been dark when I first looked at my watch at 4:10.

And that's when it hit me.

I have a concussion, I said aloud. I must have been knocked out when I first fell down this slope. I must have hit my head, no telling how many times, as I rolled down these wobbling gray rocks. I've never been knocked out before. I've never been unconscious.

They say if you've had a blow to the head, you're supposed to stay awake. I had to stay awake. Between 4:10 and 4:45, I must have passed out. And all those other gaps in time . . . I must have been out. Now it was after six. I had to stay awake.

Someone would come for me if I could stay awake.

If I could just stay awake.

2

Back in Time

I t started last Tuesday, because I had to see Leah. I mean, I didn't *have* to see her. I just wanted to. Leah and I had become pretty good friends since she saved my life back in April. We stayed in touch through Facebook and e-mail, and every now and then she would send me something in the regular mail. One of the things she sent me was a photocopy of an article about fossil footprints.

Fossils are everywhere. No matter where you live, I'll bet you could go out right now and poke around in a creek bed and find a fossil. Fossil footprints are not everywhere. When fossil footprints are discovered, scientists from all over the world get excited—even if those footprints are discovered in Alabama.

Now you see the problem. I swore I would never go back to Alabama. I was there in April and almost got killed. I was there in June and almost got killed. Now here it was August, and Leah wanted me to meet her in Alabama.

"It'll be fun," she said in an IM. "It'll be like going back in time."

"Yeah, back in time," I wrote, "back to a time when people were shooting at me."

"Oh, come on," she said. "What are the chances that someone would shoot at you again?"

"Judging from past experience, I would say chances are good," I replied.

Seconds later the phone rang. I should have looked at the caller ID before I picked it up and said, "Hello?"

"Don't be such a baby," were the first words out of Leah's mouth.

What was I supposed to say to that?

"You need to get down here before school starts," she said. "I've been in touch with some folks from the APS, and they . . ."

"The what?" I interrupted her.

"What do you mean 'what'?" she said.

"APS? What's that?" I asked.

"The Alabama Paleontological Society," she said.

"See," I said, "there's that word again."

"Paleontological?" she said. "Paleontology is the branch of science that studies fossils."

"I know what paleontology is," I insisted. "That's not the word I'm worried about. It's that other word: 'Alabama.'"

She said again, "Don't be such a baby."

What was I supposed to say to that?

"Look," said Leah, "the APS goes out there every month, and they're always finding new trackways. You know what trackways are, don't you? Trackways are what scientists call a trail of fossil footprints."

"I know what trackways are," I said.

"And a lot of the trackways they find are from giant frogs and salamanders and things like your mom studies," she continued. "They've got this one footprint from a giant frog they call 'frogzilla.' It's, like, bigger than a man's hand. That frog must've been huge. Maybe you could bring your mom back some footprints from a frogzilla."

There was silence on the phone between Leah and me for a few seconds—silence between me and Alabama.

"Okay," I said. "I'll check with my mom and dad. I'm not sure they can afford to send me down there right now. They're spending a lot of money, you know, with my sister and me getting ready to go back to school and all."

"All you've got to do is get here," said Leah. "Some folks with the APS will put us up. We can stay with them, and I know you. You don't eat much but granola bars."

"I eat granola bars when I'm lost in the woods," I said.

"Whatever," said Leah. "You coming or not?"

"I'll do my best," I promised.

My mom thought it was a great idea. My dad thought it was a great idea. Neither one of them mentioned that being in Alabama and being shot at seemed to go together. The plans were made for me to meet Leah in Birmingham on the first Tuesday in August. I was going back in time.

Back in time to when giant frogs roamed the earth.

Back in time to Alabama.

Back in time to Leah.

And, oh, yeah, back in time to a place where people were shooting at me.

3

THE SWORD

I'm not superstitious. I don't believe a black cat running out in front of you is bad luck. You can spill salt while breaking a mirror on Friday the 13th, and it's not bad luck. Walking under a ladder is not bad luck; it's bad judgment. While I was packing for my trip, though, I couldn't help wondering about my nylon olive green pants with zip-off legs, sandy-colored nylon shirt, synthetic wool hiking socks, and waterproof leather boots. These were the same clothes I had worn back in April and back in June. I hadn't worn them since, and as I had them laid out on the bed about to roll them up and stuff them in my duffel bag, I sort-of wondered if they were bad luck. The pants had a tear in the knee and the shirt had a tear in both elbows: signs of my last two trips to Alabama.

"Afraid you won't look good for your girlfriend?" said a squeaky little voice from behind me.

It startled me. I turned around to see Phoebe, my little sister, standing in the doorway to my bedroom.

"She's not my girlfriend," I said.

"Then why are you so worried about what you're going to wear?" she said.

"Mind your own business," I said.

"Phoebe, stop hassling your brother," said my mom from somewhere down the hall.

"Mom," said Phoebe, "Why does Jason get to go to all of these places and not me?"

Mom came up and stood behind Phoebe in the doorway. "Jason was invited by his friend," said Mom.

"I guess I never thought of it that way," said Phoebe. "Jason has to go hundreds of miles away to find a friend. I have lots of friends right here at home."

I would have argued with her if it would have done any good. Ever since she turned twelve back in July, she thought she knew everything. "You can come along next time we go some place that has alligators," I said. "We can always use some gator bait."

"Mom," Phoebe whined. "Jason wants to feed me to the alligators."

"Nobody's going to feed you to the alligators," Mom said.

"You're mean," said Phoebe. "No wonder you have to go hundreds of miles away to find friends." And with that she spun around and disappeared down the hall.

I turned back to my packing. I held up my pants to fold them so I could roll them up when my mom said, "You know, you've grown almost an inch this summer. Those pants might not fit you anymore."

I held the pants at my waist. They did seem a little shorter than they used to.

"And they've got a hole in the knee," said Mom. "Maybe we need to see about getting you another pair."

When she said that I had this weird feeling. I had been wearing these pants when I was shot at in the longleaf forest. I had been wearing them when I was shot at on Monte Sano Mountain. Both times I lived to tell about it. Maybe these were my *lucky* pants.

"These will be okay," I said. I rolled them up and put them in my duffel bag.

"Rachel," my dad spoke Mom's name from down the hall. There was a serious, matter-of-fact tone to his voice when he said it.

Mom turned as Dad walked past her into my room. He pushed my duffel bag to one side and sat on the bed. He looked me in the eye and then turned to my mother. His face had that matter-of-fact seriousness.

He turned back to me and said, "I just got off the phone with Deputy Pickens."

Deputy Pickens was Leah's father. He was going to be driving her to Birmingham, picking me up at the airport, and then taking us to stay with our hosts from the Alabama Paleontological Society. No big deal that he would be calling my dad—except for that tone in Dad's voice and the look on his face.

Dad took a deep breath and let it out as he said, "Carl Morris has escaped from prison."

Carl Morris has escaped from prison.

The words hung in the air like the Sword of Damocles.

According to the Greek legend, a man named Damocles wanted to know what it was like to be king, so the king prepared a big banquet for him. During the banquet, Damocles looked up to see a sword hanging over his head. The sword was held by a single horsehair. The king explained that this is what it's like to have riches and power: it's like having a sword hanging over your head. Damocles went running from the room.

We studied the legend of the Sword of Damocles a couple of years ago when I was in the seventh grade. I never thought it would have any meaning for me until I heard the words *Carl Morris has escaped from prison.* Carl Morris did his best to hunt me down and kill me back in April. I felt pretty good about him being in jail. Now that he was loose . . . it was like a sword hanging over my head. Unlike Damocles, I could not run from the room.

4

THIRD PERSON

No one said a word.

Mom had been leaning against the door frame. She stood up straight and crossed her arms, standing in the doorway with a body language that said, *You're not leaving this room*. Dad remained seated on the bed and staring straight at me. I had this urge to look up and see if there was a sword hanging over my head by a single horsehair. Instead, I rolled up my shirt and placed it in my duffel bag.

"Does this mean Deputy Pickens will not be able to pick me up at the airport?" I said.

Dad didn't answer right away. He looked toward my mom. Out of the corner of my eye I could see her return his stare.

"Carl Morris escaped? What about his brothers?" Mom said.

"Just Carl," said Dad. "The brothers are still in jail."

I folded my socks and placed them in the bag.

"You still want to go?" asked my dad. It was not so much a question for me as it was for my mother. His eyes remained on her.

Before Mom could answer for me, I said, "Yes, sir, I want to go."

I turned to my mom as she uncrossed her arms and placed her hands on her hips. "Jason," she said, "I don't know."

"As long as Deputy Pickens will meet me at the airport," I said, "I would still like to go."

At that moment I felt a buzz in my pocket. It was my cell phone. Dad had bought me one after our trip to Huntsville back in June. I pulled the phone from my pocket, and there was a text from Leah.

"U heard?" was all the text said.

I slipped the phone back into my pocket.

"The deputy said he would meet you in Birmingham if you still want to go," said my dad.

"Robert, I don't know if that's such a good idea," said my mom.

"Rachel," said Dad, "if Carl Morris wanted to find Jason, he would have a lot better chance of finding him here at home than at some obscure fossil site in Alabama."

It was the wrong thing to say.

"What do you mean, *if Carl Morris wanted to find Jason?*" Mom exclaimed. "Did he threaten him? Did he say something?"

"No," said Dad. "No. No one heard him threaten Jason or Leah or the deputy or anyone else. He just wanted us to know—Deputy Pickens just wanted us to know. Morris, if he's smart, is long gone. He's probably in Alaska by now."

"Smart?" said my mom. "The man's an idiot. If he were smart, he wouldn't have been in this mess in the first place."

I had to agree with my mom on that one. "Smart" is not an adjective you would use in connection with Carl Morris. The room fell silent again. Funny thing about a room of people not saying anything when every one of them wants to say something: it seems to make time slow down. Maybe my little bedroom was suspended in time. I wanted to take a peek at my watch to see if the second hand was moving. Checking the time, though, might be seen as an attempt to get my parents talking.

My pocket buzzed again. In my nobody's-saying-a-word room, we all heard it. Mom and Dad's eyes turned to me. I shrugged my shoulders. The second hand must have begun to move again.

"It's probably Leah wanting to know if Jason's making the trip," said my mom.

"What should he tell her?" asked my dad.

Strange. I was standing right there, and they were talking about me in the third person—like I was in another room.

"He'll be safe?" Mom asked.

Dad paused.

I was about to think the clock might stop ticking again when he said, "He'll be safe."

"Maybe I should talk with Deputy Pickens myself," said Mom.

"Maybe you should," Dad agreed. "It would probably make you feel better."

"You still want to go?" Mom asked.

It took a second or two for me to realize she was talking to me.

"Yes, ma'am," I replied.

"You're sure?" she said.

"Yes, ma'am," I said again.

My pocket buzzed.

"Tell her you'll meet her in Birmingham," said Mom. Then she walked over and gave me a hug. A long hug.

Dad remained seated on my bed after Mom left the room.

"There's something else I discovered when I was talking to Shirley Pickens," he said.

I chuckled. Deputy Shirley Pickens is about six-four and well over two hundred pounds. He's built like a linebacker. He carries a gun. And his name is Shirley. In all my fourteen years, I'd never met a man named Shirley until Deputy Shirley Pickens.

"If I were you," said my dad, "I would get that chuckling out of my system before I got to Alabama."

"Good idea," I agreed.

"Like I was trying to say," Dad said, "when I was talking with the deputy, I discovered that your host in Alabama is a friend of mine. He's an astronomer. His name is Curtis Carroll. We always call him C. C., but you should probably call him Dr. Carroll."

"An astronomer?" I said. "Why are we staying with an astronomer?"

"You've got something against astronomers?" said my dad the astronomer. I think he was joking.

"No," I said. "I'm used to astronomers. I just thought we would be staying with a paleontologist or geologist."

"C. C., uh, Dr. Carroll is a professional astronomer and an

amateur paleontologist," said Dad. "Tell him I said hello."
I nodded.

"And," Dad continued, "ask him to give you and Leah a little bit of his presentation on *time.*"

My pocket buzzed again.

"You should probably answer that before she gets the idea that you're not going," said Dad. "And Jason?"

"Yes?"

"You do want to go?"

"Yes, sir."

5

FRIENDS

<table>
<tr><td></td><td>???</td></tr>
<tr><td>Talking with my parents</td><td></td></tr>
<tr><td></td><td>U still going?</td></tr>
<tr><td>Yes</td><td></td></tr>
<tr><td></td><td>C u in bhm</td></tr>
<tr><td>I'll text you from the pane</td><td></td></tr>
<tr><td></td><td>Pane?</td></tr>
<tr><td>Plane</td><td></td></tr>
<tr><td></td><td>K</td></tr>
</table>

L eah was pretty good at text-talk. Me? Not so much. Most of the time I had rather just make a phone call. Maybe it's because I haven't had the phone all that long. Leah hasn't had her phone all that long either, though. Her dad got it for her after Carl Morris and his brothers chased us through that longleaf forest less than four months ago. Less than four months . . . seems like a lot longer than that.

I finished packing and set my duffel bag beside the bed. For a moment I stood there not knowing what to do with myself. I had just passed up the perfect opportunity *not* to make the trip. The truth is I didn't think Carl Morris was as stupid as everyone thought he was, so I didn't think he would come looking for me even if I had punched him in the face with an axe.

And then there's "the greater truth," as an old friend of mine would say. The greater truth is that I wanted to see Leah.

Much as I hate to admit it, my sister was sort-of right: I don't have a lot of friends around here. It's not my fault. All of my friends are like a year older than me. That was fine until I got to the eighth grade. Then they all went to high school, and I got left behind.

There's something else, too. When I try to tell them around here about being shot at in a longleaf forest and then again on a mountaintop, they look at me like I'm crazy. Can't blame them. I still have a hard time believing it myself. Anyway, I'll be in high school this coming year, so, who knows, maybe we'll be friends again.

6

EVIDENCE OF LIVING

On the flight to Birmingham, I reread some of the first article Leah sent me about the fossil site. The article described the discovery of fossil footprints at a coal mine by a man who was, at the time, a middle school science teacher in Oneonta, Alabama. His name was Ashley Allen.

Here is an excerpt from the article.

. . . That fall, early in the school year, Ashley Allen was orienting his Oneonta, Alabama class to the year ahead when one of his students did something unusual for a seventh grader: he volunteered. Mr. Allen mentioned that he hoped to take a fossil hunting field trip during the year and that coalfields were often good spots for finding fossils. Student Jessie Burton volunteered that his grandmother owned a coal mine.

"It was significant that Jessie's grandmother owned the mine and the mining company," says Ashley Allen. "She was able to give me permission to scout the property—no bureaucracy, no red tape, no lawyers limiting liability."

Delores Reid, Jessie Burton's grandmother and owner of

the New Acton Coal Mining Company, made the arrangements for Allen to visit the Union Chapel Mine a few miles south of Jasper, Alabama. Billy Orick, Permits Manager for the mining company, met Allen on the fringes of the site and drove him to the top of a ridge that overlooked what was then a working strip mine.

Allen was a bit overwhelmed as he stepped from Orick's truck. He thought he had come prepared in his fossil hunting regalia: wide brim hat, safari vest, trekking boots. In one hand he held a hammer, in the other, a chisel. He stood alone at the top of the ridge, surveyed the site and wondered. To the south and east the ground fell away from him at a steep angle for more than a hundred yards. Then it plunged into a gully for another thirty or so feet. From the bottom of the gully, a sheer rock wall shot straight up more than one hundred feet. Orick had told him the mining crew had seen more fossils at Union Chapel than at any other of their mining sites, but Allen wondered if this site might be too treacherous for his students. Piles of jagged rocks—the spoils of strip mining—littered the landscape that dropped away before him.

Allen drew a deep breath and took his first tenuous steps down into rocks that had not seen the light of day for more than 300 million years. Beneath his feet the rocks wobbled and slipped with every move. He could not lift his eyes from the ground beyond each step he would take. But it was enough. There in the bright, autumn sun he saw it. His fossil hunter's dream: evidence of living.

As a kid growing up in Florida, Allen made his first fossil find in high school. It was a shark's tooth. Shark teeth are not uncommon, as fossils go in the southeastern U.S., but this one was Allen's treasure—there's something about holding a relic in your hand that is millions of years old. When he entered Livingston University (now the University of West Alabama), he took his treasure with him. At Livingston, he took his prized possession and showed it to geology professor Richard Thurn. It would have been easy for Professor Thurn to dismiss so common a find as a shark's tooth. Perhaps it was Allen's enthusiasm, perhaps Professor Thurn is a great teacher, probably both, but the professor seized the opportunity. He encouraged the young student to keep looking. Alabama is one of the most fossil-rich areas of North America, he told Allen. And then he threw out a challenge.

"Fossil footprints," said Thurn. "Fossil footprints are among the great quests of geologists and paleontologists across the globe. In the footprints of ancient creatures you find more than evidence of their having lived; you find evidence of living."

The professor's words inspired Allen to change his minor from chemistry to geology. He continued his major in biology and became a high school science teacher. Teaching in Oneonta, north of Birmingham, put him in the heart of Alabama coal mining country. And it put him within an easy drive of the Birmingham Paleontological Society (BPS). As a regular member of the BPS, Allen continued in the love of fossil hunting inspired by Richard Thurn.

Professor Thurn's words resonated in his mind as Allen gazed down upon his first discovery at the Union Chapel Mine, "Evidence of living." There they were: tracks. Tracks from millions and millions and millions of years ago. Ashley Allen shouted out an exclamation that in modern times might only be uttered by a high school teacher. He shouted, "Yahoo!"

This initial evidence of daily life in the 312-million-year-old Alabama rock came in the form of invertebrate tracks. Within minutes of his first find, Allen discovered another invertebrate trackway. Moments later, a long, flat, layered rock caught his eye. He placed his chisel between the layers and with a simple pop of his hammer the rock opened up. Drawing back his tools, Ashley Allen knew beyond all doubt he was someplace special. There, revealed before him, were three distinct tracks of footprints made by ancient amphibians, and a world once lost was newly found.

The pilot announced that we were beginning our descent into Birmingham, and we should put our seat backs and trays in the upright position. The fall through the clouds was bumpy, and when we dropped out beneath them it looked like we were right on top of the airport. I could see the terminal. Leah would be in there somewhere. I wondered if she was watching the plane fall from the sky and bounce twice across the runway.

7

LEAH

As soon as the flight attendant said we could, I turned on my cell phone.

A text popped right up.

U landed?

Yes. At back of plane. Make take awhile.

Make?

Might take awhile

Come straight down concourse

You there?

At top of stares

Stares?

Stairs

Because I was at the back of the plane, I had plenty of time to text my mom and dad and let them know I was on the ground. Mom texted me to call her when we got to our host's house. After about ten minutes I was able to sling my backpack over my right shoulder and leave the airplane.

Our gate was at the furthermost point down Concourse

B at the Birmingham-Shuttlesworth International Airport. It was, I'm guessing, at least two hundred yards from the gate to the terminal. About halfway down, you could see people waiting beyond the security checkpoints. When I was about seventy-five yards away, I thought I spotted her. When I was about fifty yards away, I was sure of it.

She was looking right at me.

I stopped and shifted my backpack from my right shoulder to the left.

She was looking right at me.

Even from fifty yards, I could tell her hair was a little longer. She was wearing blue jeans. Not the cut-off jeans she wore in the longleaf forest—these were long pants. She wore a short-sleeved black blouse, and her dark hair seemed to blend into the shirt from my distance.

She was looking right at me.

I shifted my backpack back to my right shoulder and continued down the concourse.

A voice over the intercom said something about not leaving bags unattended. It sounded muffled, like it was off in a soon-to-be-forgotten dream. I paused and closed my eyes for a second. The one clear sound I could hear was that of my own pulse pounding in my ears. I opened my eyes and at that instant felt a little queasy.

She raised her left hand just above her head. I nodded toward her. She lowered her hands and head, and a second later my phone buzzed.

U ok?

I did not text her back. I nodded in her direction. Another buzz.

Y U just standing there?

This time I did text back.

Hungry. Just airplane peanuts for three hours.

I cinched my backpack up on my shoulder and continued on down the concourse.

She was, like she said she would be, at the top of the stairs—sort of. The stairs, it turns out, were escalators separated from the concourse by a rail and by the TSA. When I got to the point that I would have to go down to the baggage claim area, she called out to me.

"Meet you at the baggage claim," she said.

She swirled around and her hair did that thing where it seems to drift up in slow motion. Never seen anything like it.

I took the escalator down, and there she was at the bottom waiting for me. We stood there looking at each other for either two or three seconds or two or three hours.

"Glad you could make it," she said.

And then she stepped toward me. I was afraid she was going to hug me. Instead she smacked me in the shoulder with a sideways fist. My stomach did a somersault.

8

DOUBLE NEGATIVE

It's easy to remember a man named Shirley who's built like a linebacker and carries a gun. It's another thing to be standing next to him. Deputy Shirley Pickens was waiting near the baggage carrousel. He made everyone around him look small. I'm sure I got shorter as I approached him.

"Jason, good to see you," he said as he extended his hand.

"Good to see you, too," I said.

"You've grown, what—maybe an inch since we saw you in April?" he said.

"Almost," I agreed.

Deputy Pickens turned to Leah and said, "He's gaining on you, Leah."

Leah replied, "He may be taller than me someday, but he'll never catch me."

It was true. I was almost as tall as Leah, even though she's a year older than I am. It was also true that I would never catch her.

The drive from the airport to Dr. Carroll's house, according to the GPS on Deputy Pickens's dash, would take about ninety minutes. We were planning to stop and get something to eat along the way. I wanted to ask about Carl Morris and how he escaped. I just didn't know how to bring it up.

"You're probably wondering about Carl Morris and how he escaped," said Leah.

At that instant I became less interested in Carl Morris than I was in how she managed to know what I was thinking.

Leah was sitting in the front seat next to her dad. I was sitting right behind her. She turned around to face me and said, "That is what you were thinking, isn't it?"

Before I could answer, Deputy Pickens said, "In addition to all the state and local charges he was facing, there were federal charges because his crimes were committed in a national forest. He had to be transferred to Montgomery for an arraignment in federal court, and he convinced the marshals who were driving him to take the back roads around Gantt Lake. Just wanted to get one last look at the countryside before they locked him away for good, he said. Well, it's about the same distance from Andalusia to Montgomery whether you take the Interstate or not, so they thought, why not? Somewhere up above the lake, Morris talked them into letting him get out and take a leak. That's the last anyone saw of him."

Leah had been watching me as Deputy Pickens told the story. She turned around and pulled down the sun visor, then she opened the mirror on the visor and tilted her head to one side so that she could see me as she said, "Nothin' but swamp up there above Gantt Lake. I think the gators got 'im."

"It's possible," her father replied, "but not likely. Gators avoid people whenever they can."

"Well, he just disappeared somehow," said Leah. "State troopers couldn't even find him with their FLIR."

"Fleer?" I said.

"FLIR, F-L-I-R," said Deputy Pickens, "It stands for Forward Looking InfraRed. The troopers have one mounted on the front of one of their helicopters."

"It's a camera-like thing that sees heat instead of light," said Leah. "The state troopers were down there flyin' around the swamp within an hour. They shoulda seen Carl Morris."

We rode in silence for a few minutes. Every now and then I would catch Leah glancing at me in the mirror. At last she turned around to look straight at me and said, "Maybe Carl Morris ain't got no soul."

She stared at me as I pondered her words. Then she said, "Think about it, Jason. Carl Morris ain't got no soul. It makes perfect sense. He ain't got no soul, so he don't put off no heat."

"Leah?" said Deputy Pickens, "What have I told you about talking like that?"

I thought the deputy was talking about Carl Morris having no soul until he continued, "No more saying 'ain't' and no more double negatives."

"Yes, Daddy," Leah replied.

She turned around, closed the mirror, and flipped up the sun visor.

After a moment she muttered, "I still say Carl Morris has no soul."

After another moment, "Either that or the alligators got him."

And after another moment, "Maybe both. Now *that* would be a double negative."

9

THE RIGHT PLACE

"Fate, providence, destiny. So easy it would be to believe that Ashley Allen was born to discover fossil trackways at the Union Chapel Mine. Look at all the things that had to come together for him so to do."

Dr. C. C. had a strange way of talking.

"Long ago. Long, long, long ago, a thing amazing happened."

Dr. Curtis Carroll had told us we could call him C. C. He was older than my dad, so I felt strange calling him C. C. I had no problem calling him *Dr. C. C.*

"Five billion years into the deep, deep past, the ideal blend of hydrogen and helium congealed into a sphere with such mass that at its center there began a process of nuclear fusion."

He was tall, an inch or two taller than Deputy Shirley Pickens. His skin was darker than a starless, midnight sky.

"Nuclear fusion, do you know what that means?"

The fact is I did know what that meant. Sometimes, though, even if you do know everything, it's best to keep quiet. Besides, Dr. C. C. was doing a much better job of telling the story than I ever could.

"Nuclear fusion: that means this stuff, this hydrogen and helium that had been adrift in the coldest, darkest space, came together with such force that there was created light."

Dr. C. C. had an odd accent, and sometimes his nouns, adjectives, and verbs didn't line up the way I'm used to hearing them.

"Energy was created out of matter ... can you imagine?"

Leah sat up straighter. She and I were sitting next to each other on the sofa in Dr. C. C.'s living room. She was to my right, and Dr. C. C.'s wife, Charlotte, was sitting to her right. The others were in various chairs around the room. Dr. C. C. was standing as he spun his tale.

"It was darkest dark. It was coldest cold. And then there was light and heat."

Leah leaned forward. "The sun," she said. "You're talking about the sun."

"Very good, child," said Dr. C. C.

Child? There was something in the way he said "child." It sounded more like "chil" with a long "i" sound and no "d." Sometimes Dr. C. C. sounded South African, sometimes British, sometimes Jamaican, sometimes none of the above.

"And the good news for Ashley Allen and for you and for me is that from this mass of matter that coalesced into life-nurturing light there was enough stuff left over for there to be planets and moons. One of those planets had the fortune to be located in the circumstellar habitable zone. Do you know what that means, child?"

Leah said, "Well, I know what habitable means. A habitable zone would be a zone, or a place, where things could live. Circumstellar . . . that sounds like it might have something to do with a star . . . circum . . . means around . . . I think. So circumstellar would mean around a star . . . so circumstellar habitable zone would be a place around a star where things could live."

"Very good, child," said Dr. C. C.

I said, "The earth, third planet from our star, is in the circumstellar habitable zone, and our entire solar system is in the galactic habitable zone. We are somewhere between twenty-five and thirty thousand light years from the center of the Milky Way galaxy, and it's doubtful life could exist outside of that range."

Leah turned and gave me a look I had seen back in April when we were in the longleaf forest. It was a look that said, "You're a know-it-all."

Maybe I was showing off a bit. I just couldn't sit there and let them think I was asleep on the couch.

"Excellent, Jason," said Dr. C. C.

He called me Jason and not child. I liked that. I just wish I could figure out what accent he was using when he said it.

"So," Dr. C. C. began again, "we here on earth are at the right place in the galaxy. We are at the right place in the solar system. But who can tell me the one other place we had to be so that everything would be oh so right?"

Dr. C. C. brought his large hands together at about chest level and fanned his fingers. He let his hands drift apart.

They seemed to float about the room in opposite directions as if seeking an answer in the air.

I fixated on his left hand as it hovered between me and two people sitting side by side in chairs across the room. My focus shifted, and those two people became clear. That's when it hit me.

I laughed. And I laughed. And I laughed. And I laughed. I laughed so hard I had to squeeze my belly. I thought I was going to die.

Leah jumped up and stared down at me.

"What is wrong with you?" she said.

I laughed harder.

Through my tears I could see that Dr. C. C. had crossed his arms. He did not look happy that I had destroyed his story.

"Dr. C. C.," I struggled to say, "I'm sorry . . ." And then I laughed some more.

I clenched my eyes shut and tried to get control of myself.

No one said anything. With my eyes closed I imagined them looking at me—wondering if I had lost my mind. After what seemed like forever, my laughs became gasps for air. I had laughed myself right out of breath.

I opened my eyes, sat up straight on the sofa, and said, "Please, forgive me."

Across the room, Deputy Pickens leaned back in his chair and folded his arms high across his chest. "Well, Jason," he said, "I was wondering when it would get to you."

I almost laughed again. Something in the deputy's stern look and folded arms stopped me. Saved me.

The deputy released his arms and his stern look. He turned with a smile toward the man sitting to his left.

"Ashley?" Deputy Pickens said to Ashley Allen, "It's tough, sometimes, isn't it?"

"Yes, Shirley, it is," said Ashley Allen.

Charlotte Carroll chuckled. Leah was still standing over me. She turned toward her father and chuckled. I knew better than to even start with a chuckle.

Dr. C. C. raised his hands, this time palms up, and said, "What?"

From her end of the sofa, his wife said, "Ashley? Shirley? Look at them."

Dr. C. C. shrugged his shoulders.

His wife continued, "And look at you. You're almost two meters tall and your name is Carroll. And it doesn't help that you call yourself C. C. How many times have you shown up and they were expecting a woman?"

At that point everyone laughed—except me. I was afraid if I started again I would never stop.

When everyone else stopped, I said, "Dr. C. C., may I answer your question?"

"You can try, Jason," he replied.

I gave it my best shot, "We live in the galactic habitable zone: just the right place in the galaxy. We live in the circumstellar habitable zone: just the right place in the solar system. And . . ."

I paused for dramatic effect.

"And—I'm not sure what you would call it—I just know that we live at the right place in time."

10

GOODBYES

It turns out I was right.

Dr. C. C. seemed downright shocked that I had gotten the answer he was looking for. Everyone else looked at me with similar disbelief. I tried to be humble.

"I believe we live at the right place in time—a habitable place in time," I said. "I'm not sure what you would call it."

"Epochal habitable zone," said Dr. C. C. "That's what I call it."

Epochal habitable zone. Yeah, that sounded like the kind of mouth-mumbling phrase a scientist would come up with.

Ashley Allen stood up.

"Well, now that that's settled," he said, "I'd better hit the road. It's a long drive back to Oneonta, and I've got to get up early to meet all of you at the Minkin site in the morning."

"The what?" Leah and I said at about the same time.

Mr. Allen gave us that look schoolteachers get when they can't believe you don't know something.

"I thought we were going to the Union Chapel Mine," I said.

"Oh," said Mr. Allen. "The Minkin site . . . yeah, it was the Union Chapel Mine, and some people still call it that, but when the state took over they changed the name to the Steven C. Minkin Paleozoic Footprint site."

Allen's voice trailed off as he said, "Steve Minkin was a good friend . . ."

The way he said "*was* a good friend" told me that Steven C. Minkin would not be at the site with us except, maybe, in spirit.

Charlotte Carroll said, "Steve Minkin was a good friend to everyone in the Alabama Paleontological Society."

Deputy Pickens stood up next to Ashley Allen. It made for an interesting sight. The deputy was about half a foot taller than the schoolteacher. The deputy had all of his hair on his head. The schoolteacher had most of his hair under his chin, which is to say he had a bald head and a bushy beard.

"Me, too," said the deputy. "Better be going. Long drive back to Andalusia."

I felt a slight twist in my stomach. The idea that Deputy Shirley Pickens was not going to be around made me a little uneasy. I cut a quick glance at Leah. She seemed a little fidgety, too.

She walked over and gave her dad a long hug. She whispered something to him that I could not hear.

The deputy whispered something to her that I did hear. He said, "Don't worry, little girl, there's no way he could know where you are."

He released his daughter and said, "I'll be back up to get you kids in a couple of days."

"And Jason," he said to me, "you look after my little girl."

He gave me a smile.

Leah turned and gave me a smirk.

"And Jason," he said to me again, "don't worry. Leah's probably right. The gators probably got Carl Morris."

He walked over and shook my hand.

I knew he was just trying to make me feel better, and I wanted to say, *Just in case the gators didn't get Carl Morris, why don't you hang around?*

I wish I had.

11

MELLOW MASON

C arl Morris was standing over me with an axe.

"Mellow, Mason," he said.

The axe, handle and all, glowed like hot coals.

"Mo mood mo mee mou," said Carl Morris.

The right side of his face was swollen to the size of a softball—a purplish softball streaked with reds and blues and greens.

"Mhy mon't mou mome mith me?" he said.

It had been four months since I jabbed him in the face with that axe, and he hadn't healed yet. Yellow streaks of drool dribbled out of the right side of his mouth as he struggled to talk.

"Mit mill me mun," he said in a slow, deliberate tone as if he wanted to be sure I heard every single word.

I heard every word. I couldn't understand any word.

"Mome mon, Mason," he said and reached out with one hand.

I was about to tell him I couldn't understand a word he was saying when something twisted my foot.

I yelped.

"Shhhhh," came a voice from the dark. "You'll wake the whole house."

"You sat on my foot," I said.

"Well, get your big feet out-a the way," she said. By that time I was awake enough to realize it was Leah.

"I'm sleeping here," I said, "I was trying to sleep, anyway."

"Yeah, well," said Leah, "this is a couch. It ain't a bed."

"Tell you what," I said. "Tomorrow night you can sleep on the couch, and I'll take the guest bedroom. Maybe I'll come in the middle of the night and sit on your foot."

"Shut up about the foot," she said, "and keep your voice down."

I looked around the room for a clock. There was none that I could spot. My watch was hanging from a belt loop on my jeans, which were draped across a chair on the other side of the room. That's when it dawned on me that I was in my underwear. I made sure the covers were tucked around me.

"Pull your feet up so I can sit down," Leah commanded.

I did, and she did.

She sat in silence. It was so dark in the room that I couldn't see her face. Sitting there in the quiet and the dark, my dream about Carl Morris began to creep back into my thoughts.

"So what's up?" I said.

I didn't want an answer so much as I wanted to forget my dream.

"Couldn't sleep," Leah said.

She drew in a deep breath and let it out. Even though I couldn't see her face, I remembered the look. She would have that look she got when she was about to say something she didn't want to have to say.

"You tell anybody about this and I'll kill you," she said.

I didn't say anything. We both knew I believed her.

"Something's been botherin' me," she said.

"Yeah, me, too," I said. "I don't think your dad believes the alligators ate Carl Morris. I think he was just saying that to make us feel better."

"What's Carl Morris got to do with it?" she said.

"That's not what's bothering you? He's out there somewhere. Right?"

"I don't care about a Morris, Carl or otherwise," said Leah.

"So what's the problem?" I said.

"You tell anybody about this and I'll kill you," she repeated.

"Agreed," I agreed.

"Look," she said, "that business about being here on earth at the right place in the galaxy and at the right place in the solar system . . . I get that."

She paused.

"So?" I said.

"So the earth is the right distance from the sun and the right distance from the center of the galaxy . . ." she said.

"That's it. You've got it. Can we go back to sleep now?" I said.

I didn't want to go back to sleep. I wanted to go to the bathroom. I just didn't have my pants on.

"Shut up and listen," Leah insisted.

I tucked the covers a bit tighter around myself.

She continued, "I can understand how we can be at the right place in space, but the right place in time? How can time be a place?"

Being the son of an astronomer can work for you; it can work against you. Sometimes people expect you to know things because your dad's an astronomer. The problem is you don't always know them. Lucky for me this was one of the things I did know a little something about—enough, at least, to make it sound good.

"Think of it this way," I said. "Astronomers, cosmologists, physicists, they all believe it's been about 13.7 billion years since the beginning of our universe. So, the earth is eight light minutes from the sun. We are somewhere between twenty-five and thirty thousand light years from the center of the galaxy. And the distance from creation is 13.7 billion years."

"And 13.7 billion years or so is the right amount of time for life to develop?" Leah asked.

"That's what Dr. C. C. seems to think," I replied.

"Whatta you mean, 'that's what Dr. C. C. seems to think?'" Leah said. "You're the one that answered his question."

"Yeah, well, it's his theory," I said.

"So you were sayin' what you thought he wanted to hear?" Leah said. "I can't believe you, Caldwell. And I can't believe I came in here thinking you might know what you were talking about."

"Well, he said I was right, didn't he?" I said.

"You were bluffing," she said. "You got lucky."

"Luck had nothing to do with it," I insisted.

"Luck had everything to do with it," she said. "And you're lucky everybody's asleep right now, or I would tell 'em all about it."

She stood up, and I felt a rush of air as she spun around and walked away in the dark.

Her footsteps came to an abrupt halt.

She said, "And Caldwell . . ."

"What?" I said.

"Put some pants on."

12

Silly Hats

The first things you notice about a field full of fossil hunters are the silly hats. Fossil hunters spend a lot of time in the sun, and they like to carry their shade with them on their heads. I counted nine members of the APS—Alabama Paleontological Society—scattered among the rocks. Every one of them had on a different style of hat, and nobody was trying to make a fashion statement. There were two other members up on the ridge setting up a large, blue canopy. They, too, wore their own special versions of silly hats. I imagined that to get to know one of these people you didn't need their name; you could just call them by their hat.

"Amazing, isn't it?" said Leah.

"Yeah," I said, "I didn't realize they made so many varieties of crazy hats."

She was standing to my right. She turned and took the bill of my cap with her right hand and used it to turn my head toward her.

"What are you talking about?"

"The hats. Have you ever seen so many silly hats?" I said.

Leah said, "You're standing at one of the most important sites in the world for fossil footprints that are more than 300 million years old, and you're looking at hats?"

She had a point.

She took my hat off my head and held it out at arm's length so we both could admire it. At least I thought we were going to admire it.

"An hour in the sun with this thing and you're gonna wish you had a silly hat," she said.

She had a point.

It didn't occur to me until that moment that my black NASA cap—good-looking as it was—would be hotter than hot after a short time in the Alabama August sun. Leah slapped it back on top of my head and reached up and adjusted her own cap. It was the Baltimore Ravens cap I had sent her back in May. It was white with a purple Raven on the front.

"Thanks for the white hat," she said.

She took a red bandana from around her neck, took off the cap, spread the bandana across her head so that it draped down the back, and put her cap back on. Just like that she took the beautiful Baltimore Ravens cap and turned it into a silly hat.

She looked at me and grinned. I knew better than to mention silly hats again. It was not going to be easy, though, because at about that moment Dr. C. C. walked up and stood next to Leah. On his head was what looked like an upside-down flowerpot with a wide brim.

"So, Jason, what do you think?" said Dr. C. C.

I assumed he was not talking about the upside-down flowerpot on his head.

I said, "It's just the way it was described in that article Leah sent me." And then I paraphrased from the article, "From where we're standing on this ridge, we're looking sort of southeast, so this slope runs over a hundred yards before it drops off into that gully. That rock wall rising out of the gully is about a hundred feet high. Is that right?"

"Very good," said Dr. C. C. When he said "good" it sounded like he had three too many vowels: like "goooood."

"A couple of things I don't remember from the article," said Leah. "These furrows . . . it looks like a farmer's field that's just been plowed with a really, really, really big plow."

She was right. The giant furrows ran parallel to each other and perpendicular to the ridge where we stood. They ran all the way down to the gully where they had to stop.

"Are these furrows from the strip mining?" I asked.

"No," said Dr. C. C. It sounded like "Noooo."

"The strip mining is long done here," he said. "The state comes in periodically and turns over the ground with heavy equipment."

"Why would they do that?" I asked.

"So they can turn up new layers of fossils," Leah said.

"Very good, child," said Dr. C. C., sounding like "very goooood chiiil."

"There was something else?" Dr. C. C. asked Leah.

"Looking at the highwall," said Leah, "there on the right side, it's a little hard to tell from here, but it looks like big, gray rocks just poured down from the top of the wall."

"Spoil from the strip mining," said Dr. C. C.

"It looks treacherous," I said.

"Indeed," said Dr. C. C.

"The rocks seem to flow from the top of the highwall and cascade down like some sorta waterfall made of rocks," Leah said.

"Hard to believe this used to be a swamp," I said.

"That was a long ago time," said Dr. C. C.

"A long, long, long time ago," I agreed.

"Yes," said Leah. "but if this hadn't been a swamp millions of years ago, there wouldn't be any fossil footprints to find out here."

"True, child," said Dr. C. C.

Leah said, "Kinda makes you wonder, doesn't it Caldwell? Wonder if 312 million years from now they'll find the footprints of Carl Morris in the swamps up above Gantt Lake."

"Thanks," I said with all the sarcasm I could manage, "I'd forgotten about Carl Morris. I appreciate you reminding me."

A vehicle coming up behind us interrupted our speculations about the highwall, ancient swamps, and the fossilized footprints of Carl Morris. We all turned to see a van bouncing up the hill and leveling off as it made its way along the ridge toward us. The driver was wearing a silly hat, which I did not recognize. I did recognize the beard. It was Ashley Allen. In the van with him were several hatless heads. The van came to a halt and was engulfed by a cloud of dust that had been trailing it. Mr. Allen and his passengers waited for the dust to settle before they opened their doors and began filing out one by one. They were students from Oneonta High School.

Back when he discovered the fossil site, Ashley Allen was teaching middle school science. Now he taught at the high school, and today he had five students with him: two boys and three girls. I realized as I watched the kids climb out of the van that I would be the youngest kid out there—I wouldn't start high school for another two weeks. None of them seemed all that interested in me anyway. They were all looking at Leah. They pretended not to. They shuffled their feet and looked around as if there was nothing to see. It was obvious, though. They were all trying to sneak a glance at Leah.

I felt like the Invisible Man.

"Okay, everyone, listen up," came a teacher-sounding voice.

Mr. Allen walked around from his side of the van. He wore a wide-brimmed, Australian outback style hat and a safari vest. The article I had read mentioned a safari vest. I wondered if it was the same one even though the article had been written many years ago.

"Reckon that's the same vest?" Leah whispered into my ear.

When she did, both of the guys in Mr. Allen's group looked at me with scowls on their faces. I'll bet they didn't even know they were doing it.

I whispered back, "I was just wondering the same thing?"

More scowling.

Maybe I wasn't so invisible after all.

"Make sure you put on sunscreen and wear your hats," said Mr. Allen, "That goes for you, too, Lyndsey."

A red-haired girl, who must have been Lyndsey, shrugged her shoulders. I could see why she might not want to wear a hat. Her hair was ... well, there was lots of it. Not like she had big hair, there was just a lot of it. It seemed to be less of a covering for her head and more of a frame for her face. And it glowed. I mean ... I said it was red ... that's not quite right. It was like some exotic new color that the Hubble Space Telescope might have spotted in a distant pillar of interstellar plasma ...

"Take a picture; it'll last longer!" said Leah. And she was not whispering.

The group of five all turned to look at me, then at Leah, then back at me. I raised my right hand and made a slight wave.

I said, "Hi, my name is Jason. This is Leah. Whatever you do, don't make her mad."

13

Uncommon

Within fifteen minutes I found my first fossil.
Before we started, Ashley Allen passed out
chisels and hammers. Then he had us gather
around him for a safety-first speech. The Oneonta kids
looked as if they'd heard it all before, and they were paying
more attention to Leah than to their teacher. I was kind of
checking them out while they were ignoring me to watch
her. Leah may have been listening, or she may have kept her
attention on Mr. Allen as a way of ignoring the rest of us.
When Mr. Allen was finished, the three Oneonta girls left
together. Leah took off like she knew where she was going,
and I followed her. The two guys lingered behind.

Leah paused at the top of one of the giant furrows running downhill from the ridge. I figured she had chosen it
because there were no other fossil hunters working in it
at the time. I stood behind her and watched as she glided
down into the furrow and across the gray rocks that littered the ground. I thought back on the article I had read
about Ashley Allen discovering the site. "Beneath his feet
the rocks wobbled and slipped with every move," said the
article. Leah seemed to have no problem.

I stepped down into the piles of jagged rocks and fell flat on my butt. A pain shot down my left leg and up my left side. The pain stopped in my toes and my teeth, turned around, and met back at my butt. I clenched my jaw to keep from screaming and took a quick look around. The two guys were in the next furrow over—no doubt so they could keep an eye on Leah. They could not have cared less what happened to me. All of the other fossil hunters that I could see from the hole I was in were busy with their hunting. *Oh, well,* I thought, *at least I didn't embarrass myself in front of anyone.*

"You all right?" came a voice from on high.

I turned and looked up to see Ashley Allen standing on the ridge above me.

"He's okay. He's always gettin' himself banged up one way or another, but he always lives to tell about it," said a voice from below me. It was Leah. I turned around as she extended a hand to help me up.

Mr. Allen said, "Jason, you might want to stick with your friend. She seems to know her way around these rocks."

"Yes, sir," I said. "Thanks."

Leah helped me to my feet, and I watched as she glided down into the furrow and stopped about thirty yards from where I stood.

"How does she do that?" came the voice from on high.

I turned and gave Mr. Allen a shrug of my shoulders as a way of saying, "I have no idea."

"Be careful, Jason," he said and walked away.

A few steps and I had enough confidence to believe I wasn't going to fall again. The footing was not too bad as

I got more into the furrow. I made my way down about fifteen or twenty yards and paused to survey the scene. We had been told by Dr. C. C. during the drive to the site that morning that we could expect to find fossils in two types of rocks: clay shale and gray siltstone. Standing in the valley of that giant furrow, rocks were piled up higher than I was, and they all looked gray to me. I couldn't tell one type from another.

I climbed about halfway up one side of the furrow and started picking up rocks. The first few were about the size of my hand, and they crumbled in my hand. The rocks were like those small chalkboards I remember having when I was a little kid except they weren't black. These chalkboards were gray, and they were stuck together in layers—layer upon layer upon layer. The hammer and chisel in my back pockets were supposed to help separate the layers. They didn't seem necessary; the rocks came apart on their own.

I stepped up a few more feet and looked over the top of the furrow I was in. Every now and then I could see a silly hat bob up and down in one of the other furrows. People were scattered across the landscape bending over and picking up rocks. *This is crazy*, I thought. *Who in his right mind volunteers to pick up rocks?* Then I bent over and started picking them up myself.

A chunk that was about three feet square and four inches thick caught my eye. Within those four inches must have been five or six layers, maybe more. I started trying to pull the thing apart in the middle and was about to give up and try my hammer and chisel when it opened up like an ancient book. Between the pages of this old book was the perfect record of a 312-million-year-old fern. I remembered what Ashley Allen said when he found his first fossil out here, and I muttered to myself, "Yahoo."

"What are you yahooing about?" said Leah.

Either my mutter was louder than I thought, or she's got superhuman ears.

"Come look," I said.

The fern appeared delicate even though it was imprinted in rock and had been for millions and millions and millions of years. I held it away from my body and into the light for Leah to see.

"Amazing," she said.

"What ya got?" said an unfamiliar voice.

Leah and I turned to see the two guys from Oneonta standing at the top of one side of our furrow. One of the guys was tall and skinny with short black hair under a crumpled camo boonie hat. The other was a bit shorter and stockier with short black hair, and he was standing under a white cap with a red O on the front.

Tall and Skinny said, "Ya find somethin'?"

"Fern," said Leah, "Jason found it."

"That ain't nothin'," said Tall and Skinny. "Ferns're ever'where out here."

He looked at Leah and said, "Why don'cha quit babysittin' the little kid and c'mon over here? We'll show ya how to find the good stuff."

Leah said, "Jason ain't no little kid. He's my best friend."

She said it with such authority that Tall and Skinny was at a loss for words. We all kind of just looked at each other for a minute or so until he said, "Whatever," and scampered away.

The other guy said, "Can I see?"

He slid down toward us, sending rocks rolling ahead of him. When he got into the valley of our furrow, he stuck his right hand out to Leah and said, "My name is Nathan."

She shook his hand and said, "Leah."

"Good to meet you, Leah," he said. Then he turned to me with his right hand extended and said, "Good to meet you, too, Jason."

I shifted my 312-million-year-old rock to my left hand, dusted my right on my shirt, and shook his hand.

"Sure," I said.

"Can I see?" he said.

I handed him the rock, which he cupped in both hands as if it were the most fragile thing on earth.

"Yeah, that's a good one," he said. "A seed fern from the Carboniferous."

"Ferns don't have seeds?" said Leah. She said it more as a question than a statement—like she wasn't sure. I was not used to her being unsure of anything.

"Modern ferns don't," he said, "but these coal-age ferns did. It was during that time when the first seed-bearing plants appeared on earth."

He handed the rock back to me and said, "What you've got is a fossil of one of the first plants since the beginning of time to ever produce a seed."

He made it sound like a pretty big deal.

He waved his left hand in a big sweeping motion as if to

indicate the entire fossil site. "You can find them all over the place out here," he said.

So maybe it wasn't such a big deal.

"But just because they're all over the place out here, doesn't mean they're not important," he continued. "Think about it. They may be common here, but you can't go out and pick them up just anywhere. Things that are very common here are very uncommon everywhere else."

We all took a moment to savor a long look at my uncommon fern.

"So, Jason," he said. "You're lucky to find this."

He was not looking at me or my fern when he said it. He was looking at Leah.

14

Fossil Hunting and Astronomy

Trace fossils are what they call the types of fossils that everyone is looking for at the Steven C. Minkin Paleozoic Footprint site. I always thought of fossils as dinosaur bones. The fossils at the Minkin site are as much as 200 million years older than the dinosaurs, and they're not bones. Trace fossils are footprints, trails, and burrows left behind by animals as they went about their daily lives. The imprints left by plants like my fern are not trace fossils. These ancient imprints—and there are a lot of them left by a variety of plants—give scientists a good idea of the environment the animals lived in. All of this and more we heard from Nathan. He went on and on about it. And on and on and on.

Leah didn't seem to mind, even though most of what he said Dr. C. C. had already told us. Nathan followed us around . . . well, I should say, he followed Leah around, and he was yakking the whole time. I thought he would never shut up. At about 9:30, I thought I was going to die from his constant babble and from the heat. At 10:30, I was sure of it. I had heard more than I ever cared to know about fossils from the Carboniferous, and the temperature was at

93 degrees. The sweat had so saturated my hat that when I leaned over it dripped from the bill. I had to find some shade, some water, and—though I hated to leave Leah with Nathan—I had to have some relief for my ears.

The only shade around was on the ridge under the big, blue canopy those guys had been setting up when we first arrived. I looked back up that way and realized we had wandered a couple of hundred yards downhill from the ridge. That meant it was a couple of hundred yards back up. I wasn't sure I could make it. By that time I had several more fossils to carry. I almost wished I hadn't left my backpack in Dr. C. C.'s car, except that I would not have wanted to load it up with crumbly rock. I picked up my fossils and started making my way uphill.

"See you later," I said to no one in particular.

No one in particular did not answer back.

As I approached the canopy, I noticed Dr. C. C. talking with a man and a woman I did not recognize. They were both wearing silly hats, so I assumed they were part of the APS. The woman had several sheets of paper in her hands that she appeared to be showing to the men. She passed the papers around, and everyone looked them over with an unsmiling, stony-faced look.

Stony-faced, I thought, *how appropriate for a group of paleontologists.*

One of the stony faces started moving again. "Jason, you look like you could use some rest," said Dr. C. C. "Come here up to this shade."

The others paid no attention to me. The woman collected the papers she had passed around, then she walked back toward a greenish SUV that was parked behind Ashley Allen's van. The man picked up a hammer and chisel from a table under the canopy and walked away in the opposite direction. Their stony faces remained so.

The last thirty feet or so up to the ridge were so steep I wasn't sure I could make it while carrying my fossils. I had them cradled in both arms against my belly, which didn't leave a hand free to brace myself. And I was exhausted. The heat under my black hat was baking my brain. I turned sideways and took small sideways steps up the steep slope. When I got close enough, Dr. C. C. reached out and pulled me up.

"You must so be hot under that black cap," he said.

I would have agreed with him if my mouth could have formed words. All I could do was pant.

"Ninety-three degrees it is," said Dr. C. C., "and ninety-three percent is the humidity."

Under the canopy, they had set up a long table on which sat three large water coolers with taps. Stacked next to the coolers were paper cups. There were half a dozen or so chairs, and I collapsed into one of them, my fossils still clutched to my belly with both hands.

Dr. C. C. brought me a cup of water.

"Thank you," I managed to mutter.

I leaned back so that I could free my right hand without my fossils falling and took the water. It was so cold it burned on the way down. On my second sip I held it in my mouth for a few seconds so it could acclimate to my overheated body.

"You have found trackways, yes?" asked Dr. C. C.

I pulled off my cap and pressed the cold-water cup to my forehead.

"No, sir," I said. "No trackways. No animals. All plants, I think."

"Plants are good, too," he said. "Plants give us indication of the ecosystem in which the animals lived." I hoped he was not saying that to make me feel better about not having animal tracks.

Dr. C. C. had a small cardboard box that he seemed to have produced out of nowhere. He took the fossils cradled in my left arm and placed them in the box.

"We take these to Kayem for identification," he said. He nodded his head toward my left.

I looked to see another, smaller, green canopy about fifty yards down the ridge. I don't know how I could have missed it before. Under the canopy was a table, and behind the table was a man in a chair. He seemed to be examining things on the table.

"What is a Kayem?" I asked.

"Dr. Kayem," said Dr. C. C., "Dr. Kayem is Chief of Stratigraphy for the Geological Survey.

"Chief of what?"

"Stratigraphy."

"Strrrr . . ." I tried to pronounce it myself and couldn't do it.

Dr. C. C. came to my rescue, "Stra-tig-ra-phy. Place emphasis on the second syllable."

"And stra-tig-ra-phy is?"

He said, "Stratigraphy is the study of layering in rocks, specifically the study of rock strata to determine the distribution, deposition, and age of sedimentary rocks."

I said, "And this man, Dr. Kayem, he's a Rock Doc? In other words, he's a geologist?" Geologist is so much easier to say than stra-tig-whatever-phy.

"A geologist, yes," said Dr. C. C., "and chief of the Stratigraphy Division."

"Is that him?" I nodded in the direction of the green canopy.

"Yes," said Dr. C. C. "I will take him your specimens. He is very good at identification of our fossils."

Dr. C. C. carried my fossils over to Dr. Kayem for identification. I watched as he took them from the box and laid them out on the table. He turned toward me and pointed. When he realized I was watching, he gave a short wave. I waved back. I knew the deal. The deal was that if you found fossils you had to have them identified by an expert, who, today, seemed to be Dr. Kayem. If the fossil had great scientific value, it would go to the Alabama Museum of Natural History, the Geological Survey of Alabama, or maybe to the McWane Science Center in Birmingham where it would be catalogued for future study. If the fossil was not so great, or if it was something that the museums already had a lot of, you got to keep it. You could keep it for your personal collection; you could not sell it.

I was thinking about this and thinking about how it compared to astronomy. There are so many telescopes around the world today, and telescopes in space, that more data come in than the world's astronomers can keep up with. It's good data, though, so they catalogue it and store it in computers with the idea that someone, someday will come along and study it. A museum like the Alabama Museum of Natural History works kind of like an astronomer's computer. It stores the data, and in this case the data are hundreds and hundreds of fossils.

Yeah, I was thinking how fossil hunting and astronomy compared when I had what at the time I thought was the best idea ever.

How cool would it be, I thought, *to come out here at night.*

15

COINCIDENCE

The Oneonta girls screamed.

They were several hundred yards from the canopy on the ridge where I sat. I jumped up to try and see what was going on and walked down the ridge toward the east. When I got to Dr. C. C. and Dr. Kayem's canopy, I paused.

"They must have found something good," said Dr. Kayem.

"Or a snake," I said.

"Don't find too many snakes in these rocks," said Dr. Kayem.

"Takes just one," said Dr. C. C. He may have been making a joke—it's hard to tell with scientists sometimes.

We watched as a flock of silly hats with people under them converged on the girls. As far as I could see, the only one not wearing a silly hat was Lyndsey, the girl with the abundance of interstellar hair.

I walked on toward the east and the ridge seemed to be getting higher even though I was not walking uphill. The ground below was dropping away. About one hundred more yards to the east, the ridge began to descend as it merged with the high wall. It occurred to me that you could find a way to get up on the highwall by following the ridge and doing a little climbing. I've always liked looking down from high places. I wanted to get up on that highwall and look down on the fossil site and the silly hats that populated it.

As it was, I was already higher than everyone down in the furrows. I looked back to the west and saw Leah talking with what's-his-name. He said something to her and then started toward the crowd that was convening with the Oneonta girls. Leah started back up toward the big, blue canopy on the ridge.

I watched Leah heading to the ridge-top alone. Then I looked to where far below me the group of fossil hunters converged on the Oneonta girls. Standing there at that moment, I had no idea how things were converging on me.

My dad always says he doesn't believe in coincidences. He says, "If you look deeply enough into anything that appears to be a coincidence, you can find a cause."

Cause and effect. That's the way my dad the scientist looks at things, and maybe he's right. Earlier I had seen Dr. C. C. talking with stony-faced APS members. At the moment I was thinking about climbing to the top of the highwall. I had just had the bright idea that it would be cool to come out at night. The Oneonta girls had just discovered something, though right then I didn't know what. All of these things would come together in a grand coincidence to cause an effect I could not have predicted. I could not have predicted it because there was one little bit of information I didn't have at the time: Leah's hometown newspaper, *The Andalusia Star News*, has a section they call "Neighbors."

At the time I didn't know about "Neighbors."

And at the time, I had forgotten all about Carl Morris, who, it turns out, knew all about "Neighbors."

16

CHATTER

"You had a chance to chat with your girlfriend?" That was the first thing Leah said to me when I walked up to her under the big, blue canopy. She was the only one there. Everyone else was down with the Oneonta girls, except for Dr. Kayem who waited under the green canopy. She slumped back in one of the chairs and pressed a paper cup against her forehead. Her white Ravens cap and red bandana rested on the arm of the chair.

I turned both hands palm-up and said, "What?"

"The little redheaded girl," she said, "you had a chance to chat her up yet?"

"Chat her up?" I said. "Since when did you start talking like you were from Great Britain?"

"I dunno," said Leah. "She's a redhead. Maybe it made me think of England or Ireland or something."

"Chat her up," she continued. "Has a nice ring to it, don't you think? Sounds sorta musical. Chat her up, chat her up," she sang.

"I think being out there in the hot sun with what's-his-name's constant babble has made you crazy," I said.

"His name is Nathan, and I think he's sorta cute, don't you?"

"Hadn't noticed."

"What? You mean there's something Jason Caldwell hasn't noticed? Son of two scientists, amazing powers of observation, and you haven't noticed? Maybe you were paying too much attention to that little redheaded girl."

She paused long enough to take a sip of water. I grabbed a cup for myself and filled it from one of the coolers.

"You want me to get the chat started for you?" Leah said. "I ain't as good . . . I'm *not* as good with words as you are, but I could get it started for you . . . let her know you're interested."

I squeezed my paper cup so hard that water squirted in every direction.

Leah stood up, filled a fresh paper cup with water, and handed it to me.

"Sorry," she said. "Didn't mean to upset you."

I said nothing.

She went on, "But you were sorta starin' her down this morning."

"I was just trying to figure out what color her hair is," I said.

"Yeah, it does sorta look like somethin' a space telescope woulda dragged in," she said.

I laughed.

"Something a space telescope would've dragged in," I said. "I guess that's one way to look at it."

"She's cute though, huh?" said Leah. "Want me to let her know you're interested?"

"Can we just give it a rest?" I begged.

I took a seat, and Leah sat back down. We sat in silence and watched as the gaggle of silly hats flocked together some three hundred or more yards away from us.

"Where did Dr. C. C. go?" Leah asked.

"Isn't that him down there with the upside-down flower pot on his head?"

"See?" she said. "That's what I'm talkin' about. You have great powers of observation. Who else would've described it as an upside-down flower pot, but that's exactly what it looks like."

We went back to our silence and watched.

After ten minutes or so, the upside-down flowerpot started to move our way. Soon it was followed by a string of other hats. It was hard to be sure at that distance what was going on.

"Looks like Nathan and that skinny kid are trying to carry something," said Leah. "And it looks like Mr. Allen and a couple of the APS guys are trying to help."

I agreed. "Maybe we should go down there and see if we can give them . . ."

"No," Leah interrupted me. "We'd just be in the way. They got more help than they need as it is."

"Well, let's do something," I said. "I don't want to look like I'm just sitting here taking it easy while someone else does all the work."

"But you are just sitting here taking it easy while someone else does all the work," she said.

"Yeah, well, I don't want to look like it," I repeated.

We stood up and made our way over to the green canopy

where we introduced ourselves to Dr. Kayem. He asked us to help him clean off his table.

"Looks like they're bringing up a rather large slab," he said. "We'll need room on the table."

Almost all of the fossils we moved from the table were ferns of some form or another. There were a few with squiggly lines. Most of the squiggly lines were no more than watermarks, according to Dr. Kayem.

"But look at this one," he said.

He showed Leah and me a flat, gray slab about a foot long and half as wide with what looked like waves drawn across it.

"Fish trails," said Dr. Kayem. "These were made by the back fin of a fish as he swam in shallow water. You can see how the waves get closer together toward the end. That means the fish was speeding up. This is one we will keep for the museum collections."

"And it looks like we may have something else coming for the collections," he said as he looked up from the table and out over the Minkin site.

Leah and I followed his glance to watch as the guys from Oneonta and several others struggled to bring a large, gray slab to Dr. Kayem for examination.

17

How Does Who Know What?

"This may be the earliest example of herding ever discovered," said Dr. Kayem.

There were lots of "Oohs" and "Ahs." The slab discovered by the Oneonta girls was impressive. It was covered with trails of footprints all going in the same direction.

Dr. C. C. said, "This could provide persuasive evidence for group behavior in tetrapods from the Early Pennsylvanian."

The "Oohs" and "Ahs" came to an abrupt halt when he said it.

Dr. Kayem tried to interpret, "What Dr. Carroll is saying is that these are tetrapod footprints. Tetrapod is a broad term for four-footed vertebrates. We think the tetrapods at this site were salamander-like creatures, and if you look at these tracks, you see they're all going in the same direction. This could be evidence for herding."

"Like a herd of cows?" said Leah. "I never thought of amphibians as traveling in herds."

"Some do at certain times," said Dr. Kayem. "They may

migrate together, feed together, or run from predators together . . ."

"How do you know these tracks were all made at the same time?" said Tall and Skinny. I was surprised to hear him ask an intelligent question.

"This would have been a swampy area when these tracks were made," said Dr. Kayem. "Sediment would have covered the tracks very quickly in order to preserve them like this."

One of the Oneonta girls said, "He said something about Pennsylvania. We're in Alabama. What's Pennsylvania got to do with it?"

"Not Pennsylvania, Pennsylvanian," said Dr. Kayem. "The Carboniferous period lasted from about 360 million to 286 million years ago. Here in the United States we subdivide it into the Mississippian Period which lasted from about 360–320 million years ago and the Pennsylvanian Period, lasting from 320–286 million years ago."

Ashley Allen said, "The Carboniferous is one of six periods that make up what era?"

I was beginning to feel like I was back in school. And by the looks on the faces gathered under the green canopy, so was everyone else. I knew the answer; I just didn't want to perpetuate that "back to school" feeling by saying it out loud.

"Paleozoic," said What's-his-name.

"Very good, Nathan," said Mr. Allen.

Thanks a lot, Nathan, I thought to myself, *thanks for keeping us after class.*

"The Paleozoic era lasted from about 543 to 245 million

years ago," said Mr. Allen. "Who can tell me what brought about the end to the Paleozoic?"

Before What's-his-name could butt in, I said, "Mass extinctions."

"Very good, Jason," said Mr. Allen.

Out of the corner of my eye I could see Lyndsey begin to twirl her interstellar hair with one finger. Hair twirling, or so I've been told, is a sure sign a girl is bored. The other Oneonta girls took the hint and started twirling their hair.

Leah took her hat in her right hand, bent over at the waist and shook her hair over the back of her head letting it fall toward the ground. As she stood back upright, she ran her left hand through her hair. She leaned back and ran her fingers through her hair a couple of more times before standing upright and putting her hat back on.

What's-his-name and Tall and Skinny both let out a small gasp.

I think I may have, too.

"How do you know?" asked Leah. The question seemed to be directed toward no one in particular.

Tall and Skinny blushed, believe it or not. What's-his-name and I caught each other looking at each other for an instant. The Oneonta girls froze in mid-twirl.

"How does who know what?" said Lyndsey.

"The Early Pennsylvanian, Lower Carboniferous, these trackways . . . how does anyone know how old they are?" said Leah.

Dr. Kayem said, "Look at the highwall." As we did, he continued, "You can see the variations in color in the layers as you go from top to bottom. These layers mean something to a stratigrapher . . ."

"A what?" said Tall and Skinny.

"A geologist," said Dr. Kayem. "We know the age of some of the levels from radiometric dating. We estimate the age of the other levels based on their relationships to the known dates."

He paused and looked from face to face, perhaps waiting for another question.

When no questions came he said, "It's like knowing your birthday. Your birthday is a fixed date that you're very familiar with. You can relate other dates to your birthday. You know whether something came before or after, so you know if it is younger or older than you are."

He paused again.

"Questions?" he questioned.

"Yes," said Tall and Skinny. "What's for lunch?"

18

Eyes Wide Open

D r. C. C. took Leah and me to a barbecue restaurant in Jasper at about 11:30. This might not seem so unusual if not for the fact that we had packed lunches so we could eat at the fossil site. When we stepped into the restaurant I figured I knew why we were there: air conditioning. It was beautiful. Cold, fresh air swept over us as we stepped out of what was by then the near hundred-degree heat. But when Dr. C. C. told the hostess he needed a table for five, I suspected there might be reasons other than the air conditioning.

On the ride from the site to the restaurant, I had wanted to bring up the idea of coming out at night. I rehearsed my argument in my head several times. There just never seemed like a good time to bring it up, because Dr. C. C. had a look on his face . . . It's hard to describe . . . It's that look your parents get when they've got something to say, and they're not yet ready to say it. And it's a look that says, *Don't bother me right now, I'm thinking.*

Leah and I didn't say anything to each other on the ride to the restaurant, either. I guess we were too burned up and burned out from the heat. When we got there and Dr. C. C. asked for a table for five, she and I looked at one another with raised eyebrows. We took our seats at a big, round table, and before the waiter could bring our water, I saw them. It was the stony-faced man and woman I had seen Dr. C. C. talking with earlier that morning. The hostess brought them to our table.

Their names were Peggy and Calvin Branch. They were married to each other, and here's the weird part: he was a member of the APS, the Alabama Paleontological Society, and she was a member of the BPS, the Birmingham Paleontological Society.

When the waiter returned with five tall glasses of water and asked for our order, Mrs. Branch said, "Leah, Jason, order whatever you want. Calvin's buying."

The way she said it I knew that wherever Peggy Branch went, she was in charge. I couldn't help wondering how it was going to work out at our lunch table. Leah was there, and she was used to being in charge. I ordered a chicken plate, took a long drink of water, and leaned back in my chair so that I could see the whole table at a glance in case something happened.

As the waiter walked away, Peggy Branch leaned in toward the middle of the table. Mr. Branch and Dr. C. C. leaned in. Peggy Branch cut her eyes toward me, and I leaned in. When the rest of us were gathered toward the center of the table, Leah leaned in.

"This does not leave this room," Peggy Branch said in a whisper just loud enough to be heard over the din of the restaurant lunch crowd.

She shifted her eyes between Leah and me and then cut them toward Dr. C. C.

"You trust these two?" she said.

Dr. C. C. nodded.

"This does not leave this room," she repeated.

I said, "Yes, ma'am."

Leah nodded.

"Someone is stealing fossils," she said.

Her eyes widened, and without moving her head, she cut them from person to person.

"Someone is stealing fossils from the Steven C. Minkin Paleozoic Footprint Site," she said, as if we hadn't already guessed where the fossils were being stolen from.

Her eyes got even wider, and she seemed to be staring at all of us at once.

"Someone is stealing fossils from the Steven C. Minkin Paleozoic Footprint Site, and they are selling them on eBay."

Her eyes, already as wide as they could get, took one last spin around the table. She leaned back, and we all followed her lead.

I wanted another sip of water. I just didn't want to be the one who broke the mood of melodrama at the table. Out of the corner of my eye I saw Leah reach for her water glass.

"Do you have any idea who is stealing from the site?" Leah asked.

Peggy Branch's eyes narrowed. She said nothing.

Dr. C. C. said, "Calvin has a plan."

Leah and I both sat up a little straighter in our chairs. Somehow we both knew that whatever the plan was, it would involve us. Otherwise, why would we have been there? Why would they have been telling us these things?

Peggy Branch leaned in toward the middle of the table again. With due diligence, we all followed her in. It might have been her husband's plan, yet it was obvious Mrs. Branch was going to tell it. Her eyes widened. She looked each of us in the eye, this time turning her head without moving her eyes.

Peggy Branch said, "How would you kids like to spend the night at the Steven C. Minkin Paleozoic Footprint Site?"

19

Just Like Old Times

When I stepped out of the restroom, Leah was standing there waiting for me. "Well, Jason," she said, "looks like you were right."

During lunch, Peggy Branch had laid out the plan for catching the fossil thief. When lunch was finished, I excused myself to wash the barbecue sauce from my hands. The restrooms were down a narrow hall off the main dining room. When I stepped out, Leah was waiting.

The way she said, "Well, Jason, looks like you were right," sounded more like an accusation than a compliment.

"Aren't I always?" I said.

"No," she said.

We stood there looking at each other for what may have been a minute or two. Never seen eyes like hers. Dark, dark, dark eyes. Yet somehow full of light. I flashed back to the first time I met her just four months before. At that time she was more than an inch taller than me. Now I was about her same height. I could look straight into her dark eyes. Almost.

"Well?" she said.

I tried to say *Well, what?* when I realized I was not breathing. I drew in a deep breath.

"You all right?"

"Yeah," I said. "Too much barbecue."

And then I said, "So . . . what is it that I'm right about that I don't even know I'm right about?"

"Gettin' shot at every time you come to Alabama," she said.

For ever-so-brief-an-instant I was confused.

The instant passed.

And I knew.

Just in case I didn't know, Leah said, "How you know those fossil thieves ain't got guns?"

There was no answer to that.

"You just agreed to spend the night waitin' up for a thief or thieves—we don't know how many there might be," she said.

Nothing I could say about that, either.

"Last time you an' me spent the night together outside, three guys was tryin' to kill us."

She had a point.

"Hey," she said, "it'll be just like old times."

20

THE PLAN

Calvin Branch had a plan—a simple plan the way he described it. Dr. C. C. would take Dr. Kayem into his confidence, and the two of them would announce that they were leaving the slab discovered by the Oneonta girls at the site overnight. Their excuse would be that the discovery was too valuable to move without taking special precautions. They would claim they were coming back the next day with a crew from the Alabama Museum of Natural History to move the slab.

"It's somewhat true," said Calvin Branch. "It's very difficult to move a large slab like that without breaking it. We've all broken our share."

His wife said, "Calvin, you have certainly broken your share. Not I."

If the thief—or thieves—was among the group at the site that day, he would know that the slab would be there for just one night. He would have to make his move that night. Leah, Dr. C. C., and I would be watching the site throughout the night from the highwall. Mr. and Mrs. Branch would be staying the night at a motel a few minutes away in Jasper. When we saw something going on during the night, we could call the Branches, they would notify the local police, and they would catch the thief red-handed.

When Calvin Branch was laying out the plan at the restaurant, it all made perfect sense. Besides, it had two things going for it that interested me. One, we would be staying the night. And two, I would get to be up on the highwall. Dr. C. C. called Leah's parents and my parents to make sure they were okay with the plan.

I got something of a bonus, too. There was no good cell phone signal below the highwall, so after lunch, I was to climb up to the top and see if I could get a signal. I would follow the ridge just like I had envisioned earlier that morning. I imagined What's-his-name and Tall And Skinny trying to tag along and me having to tell them no. Lyndsey would, no doubt, be impressed.

Calvin Branch had come prepared. He had a couple of sleeping bags in the back of the greenish SUV I had seen earlier at the Minkin site.

"Probably be so hot tonight you won't need a sleeping bag, but you can use them to sit on," he said.

He also had a pair of binoculars we could use. The binoculars must have been new, because there were several pink peanuts clinging to the case. You know, those Styrofoam peanuts they use for packing.

"New binoculars?" I asked.

"No," replied Calvin Branch. "Why do you ask?"

"The pink peanuts," Leah answered for me.

Peggy Branch said, "They're everywhere. Calvin keeps a box of them in the SUV because he thinks he's going to find a slab of fossil trackways that he'll want to protect."

"Peggy," said Calvin Branch, "these people don't care about that."

"Those peanuts cling to everything," Mrs. Branch continued. "I don't know why he keeps them. He's never found a specimen worth bringing home, much less one to turn over to the museum."

"Peggy, please!" Calvin Branch pleaded.

"Now whoever has been selling our trackways on eBay is a fossil hunter. He's a thief, too, of course, but awfully good at finding fossils. As much as Calvin is out there, you would think he could figure out how to spot them."

Calvin Branch threw his hands up in the air and turned away from his wife. "Y'all want the sleeping bags?"

We took the sleeping bags and stuffed them into the trunk of Dr. C. C.'s car. Leah shook off some pink peanuts and put the binoculars in her backpack. I put the lunches we had packed and not eaten in my backpack where I already had some granola bars for backup. On the way back to the site, we stopped and picked up several extra bottles of water.

Looking back on it, we all should have known better. The State of Alabama controls the site. We should have called the state troopers or somebody and let them stake it out. It never crossed my mind that anything could go wrong, even after Leah suggested that fossil thieves might carry guns.

And besides, Dr. C. C. had called Leah's dad. If the deputy thought it was okay, who was I to be concerned? What I did not realize at the time was that because he had been driving Leah and me to Dr. C. C.'s house the day before, Deputy Shirley had not read the paper. He had no idea what the *Andalusia Star News* had said about his little girl.

21

HARD, BLACK SUNSHINE

D r. Kayem was not happy with the plan.

The way he put it was, "Only Calvin Branch could come up with an idea this dim-witted."

Calvin Branch was not standing there at the time. I got the impression it would not have mattered to Dr. Kayem, though.

Dr. C. C. tried to reassure him. "At the least," he said, "we get to spend the night under the stars."

"This was Calvin's idea, wasn't it?" said Dr. Kayem.

"It was Calvin's idea that we with the blue tarp cover the slab. That way easily we can see it through the binoculars from the highwall," said Dr. C. C.

"If that was his idea, it's the only good one he ever had," said Dr. Kayem. "But overall, I'd say this whole idea stinks. Where is Calvin now?"

"He is taking his wife to check in at the local motel," said Dr. C. C. "He will be back here to lock up after you cover the trackways."

It was at about that time that I decided I would head up to the top of the highwall to see if I could get a cell phone signal. If not, we wouldn't be staying that night, and the two doctors could stop bickering.

Leah grabbed her hammer and chisel and glided down into one of the furrows. What's-his-name spotted her and headed in her direction. The Oneonta girls were back in the same area where they had discovered their slab of trackways. Tall and Skinny was talking with someone who, judging from the hat, was Ashley Allen. No one paid any attention to me as I walked along the ridge toward the wall.

The heat was brutal. The humidity was brutal. I was wearing my backpack so that I could carry a couple of bottles of water, and I had my cell phone in the backpack. If I had tried to carry the phone in my pocket, it would have become soaked with sweat.

Following the ridge until it merged with the highwall was easy enough, considering the heat. The last forty feet up, though, I thought I would die. It was steep. I more or less crawled up using my hands and knees as much as my feet. When I got to the top, I sat down, pulled off my backpack, and downed a bottle of water. From where I sat, I'm pretty sure I was looking north. To my right was a stand of scrubby trees. To my left was the highwall. I had been told not to look over the wall. Dr. C. C. didn't want anyone to see me up there. He was afraid the fossil thief might spot me and realize what we were up to. Looking west beyond the highwall would have to satisfy my desire to look down on things.

I took out my cell phone and called home. My little sister answered.

"Phoebe," I said, "I need to speak with Mom or Dad."

"They're not here," she said.

"Where are they?" I asked.

"Out," she said.

"Out where?" I said.

"Out together," she said.

Trying to communicate with her may be the hardest thing I ever try to do.

She said, "Anybody shoot at you and your girlfriend yet?"

"She's not my girlfriend. And no, nobody's shooting at us," I said.

"Too bad," she said.

I said, "Phoebe, you don't want people shooting at me, do you?"

"That depends," she said. "Do you want to feed me to the alligators?"

I hope I didn't pause too long before saying, "No, I don't want to feed you to the alligators."

"Listen," I said, "I need you to give Mom and Dad a message, please. Tell them that Leah and Dr. C. C. and I will be spending the night on top of this high bluff at the fossil site. If it doesn't get cloudy we should get a great view of the stars."

Phoebe promised to deliver my message, and as I hung up the phone I thought I heard a muffled laugh. It sounded like it was coming from my right. I looked and could see nothing among the thick stand of scrubby trees.

Probably a crow, I thought. It didn't matter anyway; I had no intention of wandering in among these thick, weedy-looking trees.

I had accomplished the first phase of our mission: The cell signal was good. I leaned back on my elbows and gazed out to the west. A few small patches of trees dotted rolling green hills that stretched to the horizon. *How different this is from my first two trips to Alabama*, I thought. My first trip was to the longleaf forests near Leah's home around Andalusia, and there were evergreens as far as you could see. My second trip was to Monte Sano Mountain in Huntsville, which was covered with broad, leafy, deciduous trees. I wondered why this part of Alabama was not covered in trees.

To the northwest, a streak of lightning bolted from the sky to the ground. Or from the ground to the sky. It flashed so fast it was hard to tell whether it went down or up. I sat up straighter and counted while I listened. I got to sixty and never heard thunder. The lightning had to be many, many miles away. At that distance, the sky and ground seemed to merge into a mesh of gray haze. Above me the sky was blue with just a few high clouds. I knew that with the heat and humidity so high, there was a good chance of afternoon thunderstorms. They would be scattered, though, so maybe they would miss us.

Us? I thought. *There is no us up here. There's just me.*

I liked the idea of being up there by myself. I mean, I like people; it's just that sometimes I like to be left alone so I have time to think. I sat and tried to imagine what it must have been like for the creatures that lived around here 312 million years ago. This would have been a coal swamp with . . .

Coal.

That's why this area of Alabama is not covered with trees, it dawned on me.

Coal, after all, is why I was there. The Steven C. Minkin Paleozoic Footprint Site had once been known as the Union Chapel Mine. It was a strip mine, which means layer after layer after layer was removed from the surface until the miners got down to the seam of coal. The first layer to be stripped away would be the grasses and trees. When miners got to the coal and took what they could, they were supposed to "reclaim" the area. In other words, they were supposed to put everything back like they found it, which, of course, they could never do. Reclaiming meant kind of smoothing out the rocks scattered across the ground and planting grass. This explained why as far as I could see to the west, there were rolling green hills with not so many trees.

The whole business about strip mining, I had read in one of the articles Leah sent me back when she was trying to talk me into coming to the place. One thing I did not read in any of the articles was this: coal is hard, black sunshine. Sitting there in the blazing sun with the humidity around ninety percent made it easier to imagine that spot of ancient Alabama as one big swamp.

In the upper Carboniferous Period the plants were different and huge. Even the mosses and ferns could be big as trees. These coal-age plants would have absorbed the energy from the nearby star—the same star that was baking me at that moment. They stored that star's energy in their trunks and stems and branches and leaves. When they died they were covered over in the swamp and then compressed by shifting continents and millions of years of sediments piled upon sediments. In modern times a coal company came along and scraped the surface right back down to the level of that ancient swamp. When the coal was burned, it released the sunlight's energy that had been stored for more than 300 million years.

Hard, black sunshine.

I was kind of proud of myself for coming up with the idea. And I liked the way it related back to astronomy with our star, the sun. I would let Leah and Dr. C. C. in on my hard, black sunshine hypothesis that evening. In the meantime, I had to slide back down from the highwall so I could climb it again later.

22

Going to Columbus

"Do *not* let C. C. show you the way," Dr. Kayem was emphatic.

"We'll be going straight up," I said. Somehow I felt like I should be defending Dr. C. C.

"C. C. can get lost walking in a straight line," said Dr. Kayem. "You and your girlfriend know how to read a compass?"

I felt a warm rush that seemed to start at the back of my neck and flow up through my ears. It must have been the 95-degree heat bouncing up from the gray rocks.

"I'm not exactly his girlfriend," said Leah. "But both of us can read a compass. Not sure it'll do us much good, though. Like he said, we're going straight up."

"So which one of you can read a topo?" asked Dr. Kayem.

"I can," we both answered.

Dr. Kayem handed us each a photocopy of a topographical map of the fossil site, which, according to the map, is located in the Cordova quadrangle. The photocopy was black and white, faded, and somewhat difficult to see. The original color map would've been nice. I chose not to say anything about that—Dr. Kayem was in a bad enough mood already.

"And you have a compass?" he said.

"In my backpack," I said.

"Good," said Dr. Kayem. "You and your girl . . . uh, you and your friend lead the way. C. C. can find galaxies millions of light years across deep space. Here on earth he has a hard time finding his way out of a parking space."

Dr. C. C. was standing right next to me. He said, "They call it 'Going to Columbus.'"

"The first day we were to meet out at this site, C. C. wound up in Columbus, Mississippi," said Dr. Kayem. "You would think he would have known he was headed in the wrong direction when he saw the sign that said 'Welcome to Mississippi.'"

Dr. C. C. said, "My earth-bound sense of time is not so great either."

"Good point," said Dr. Kayem. "You kids need to help keep him moving in a straight line in space *and* time."

"Kayem, sad to say, is correct," Dr. C. C. agreed. "Ask me where the earth was in relation to the center of the galaxy 312 million years ago, and I can tell you. But do not ask me to meet you somewhere in four-dimensional space-time today unless you have a watch and a GPS."

Leah was smiling at Dr. C. C. when she said, "Will a topo map work instead of a GPS?"

Dr. Kayem chuckled.

"A topo will do," he said.

"As long as Jason has his compass," said Dr. C. C.

I took the compass from my backpack and hung it around my neck. I took a look at the watch attached to my belt. It said 1:30.

"You should be going," said Dr. Kayem. "Folks will be leaving here soon; it's just too hot. I'll make sure the Oneonta girls' trackways are covered in the blue tarp right where we agreed. You make sure you pull far enough off the road that no one spots your car on their way out."

We were walking to Dr. C. C.'s car when Leah said, "I'll wait here if you want to run down and say goodbye to the little redheaded girl."

I said nothing.

She put her hand on my shoulder and stopped me. She watched as Dr. C. C. walked on ahead of us. When he was several yards away, she whispered, "Doesn't this all seem sorta strange to you?"

I shrugged.

"Look at it," she whispered. "We're about to climb to the top of that highwall and sit up all night waiting for someone to come along and steal a rock."

"It's not just a rock," I protested.

"Whatever," she said. "To all the folks out here in silly hats, it's not just a rock . . . But I guess that's the answer, isn't it?"

"What?" I said. "Answer to what?"

"Well," she said, "You know my dad's a deputy. If someone called the sheriff's office and said, 'Hey, I need a stakeout on a rock,' they'd be laughed right out of Andalusia."

I was beginning to see what she meant.

"We're the only ones who can do it," I said. "To the rest

of the world, it's a rock. To the silly hats, it's history from a lost world."

"Yeah," she said, "You're right. And you know what, Caldwell?"

I shrugged.

She said, "I hate it when you're right. It usually means trouble."

23

GOING UP

"I hate not knowing where I am," said Leah.

"I hate not knowing where I'm going," I said.

"Between the two of us we could get twice as lost," she said.

We were standing in what looked like a big ditch. Dr. C. C. had pulled off the paved road onto what was not much of a dirt road. It was more of a path just wide enough for his little car. It snaked through some scraggly bushes that lined the side of the paved road. As we got further away from the paved road, scraggly bushes were replaced by scraggly trees. We bounced down into the ditch-like place, and I was surprised we didn't knock the bottom out of the car. The road or path or whatever it was blended into the ditch. We all got out and tried to get our bearings—except for Dr. C. C. He didn't even pretend to be oriented.

"I hope you two know where we are and where we are going," he said.

As one of the two, I had to agree. The unfortunate truth was we couldn't know where we were going until we figured out where we were. For a moment, I looked back and forth between my compass and my faded topographical map. I switched the map around so that it was oriented north then turned myself so that I was looking south.

"You may be foolin' yourself, but you ain't foolin' me," Leah said.

"I'm not even fooling myself," I said.

Looking south, which was more or less the direction we needed to go, we were staring into a steep bank covered with scraggly, leafy trees. The trees made it impossible to get a fix on a landmark that we could connect to our topo map.

"What we need," said Leah, "is to know exactly where we are on the map. Then we'll have a starting point that'll get us heading in the right direction."

"Perhaps the GPS in my auto will tell where we are," said Dr. C. C.

Before I could say it to her, Leah said to me, "Why didn't you think of that?"

The GPS did show where we were. Leah and I marked the spot on our maps.

"It would still be a lot easier if we had a spot in the distance we could set our sights on," I said.

"You want me to take the compass," she said. "I can follow it if it's too much for you."

I set the bezel on my compass, folded my map and stuck it in my back pocket, and took off to the southwest.

"You coming?" I said.

We had gone about sixty yards when Leah said, "We forgot the sleeping bags."

When I looked back toward her I noticed that we had lost sight of the car and of Dr. C. C.

"Too hot for sleeping bags anyway," I said.

"Need something to sit on," she said.

"I have a beach towel in my backpack," I said.

"Same one from April?" she said.

I nodded.

"And you're wearing the same clothes, except you got the legs zipped off of your pants," she said.

I nodded again.

"Hope your clothes ain't bad luck, Caldwell," she said.

Leah turned around to look in the direction we had come from.

"Yeah," she said, "Can't say I want to go back for a sleeping bag, but we really should go back for Dr. Carroll, don't you think?"

I called out, "Dr. Carroll! Dr. C. C.!"

"Here, children," came a voice from somewhere above us.

"Stay where you are, sir," I said. "Leah will come and get you."

"*Leah* will come and get you?" she said to me.

"I need to stay right here and keep us on the proper compass heading," I said.

Leah mumbled something I'm not sure I wanted to hear.

"Dr. Carroll?" she shouted.

"Yes, child?" he called.

"I'm comin', just keep talking."

I sat against a tree trunk to keep from rolling down the hill and waited. Dr. C. C. was somewhere above me spouting a steady stream of words that seemed familiar. At about the time he stopped, I realized he had been reciting the Preamble to the Constitution. I figured Leah would need me to talk her back to my location and was trying to remember the Gettysburg Address when she and Dr. C. C. came rambling in almost on top of me. I jumped up just in time for Dr. C. C. to grab onto my tree and slump down against it.

"Coming down may worse be than going up," he said.

I took a bottle of water from my backpack and opened it for him. He drank about half in one gulp.

"Did I tell you children about the time I spent in Hawaii at the Mauna Kea Observatory?" he said.

"No, sir," we both replied.

"Studying NGC 427, I was," he said.

Leah glanced at me.

"It's a spiral galaxy," I said. "Dr. C. C. is known for his work on distant galaxies."

She raised an eyebrow and turned back to Dr. C. C.

"I had just turned forty-two years old," Dr. C. C. continued.

What has this got to do with climbing this hill? I thought.

"One night, very, very late, I made a startling discovery," he said.

Somehow I knew this particular "startling discovery" had nothing to do with spiral galaxies.

"That night, very, very late, I discovered that no longer do I bounce," he said.

Leah and I exchange another quick glance. At least now we had some sense of where the conversation was going.

"Yes, children," he went on, "when one is young as you now are, one can take a fall and bounce right back. But at some point one does not bounce. For me that point came at the Mauna Kea Observatory late, late one night when I fell from the telescope."

"How can you fall off a telescope?" Leah said.

Even as the words were coming out of her mouth, I could see that she regretted having said them. It's funny. In all the time I'd spent with her, I had never seen her regret saying anything.

"My dad has some pictures of himself with one of the telescopes at that observatory," I told her. "I'll send you one. Believe me, you don't want to fall off of that telescope even if you do bounce."

"Listen," said Leah.

Down below us we could hear a series of cars going past from west to east.

"That would probably be the APS members leaving the site," she said.

"No doubt," said Dr. C. C. "We should be moving, or the trackways will not be under surveillance."

He worked his way up by holding onto the tree. It took him a couple of minutes.

"My left knee had to be repaired surgically," he said. "That was many years ago. It may be time for an upgrade. Climbing like this is so not easy. But I suppose we must carry forward."

I checked my compass bearing and resumed my climb to the southwest. Leah waited for Dr. C. C. so that he would be between her and me. Maybe that way we could keep him headed in the right direction.

For more than an hour I could hear Dr. C. C. grunting

and groaning at varying distances behind me. When the sounds seemed further away, I would stop and look back to see him and Leah pausing for a rest. It didn't look like he was in bad shape; it looked like he was in pain. With every pause he would rub his left knee while he grimaced and let out a few extra grunts and groans.

At long last we reached a point on the hill where we came out from under the trees. For the first time since we left the paved road and bounced into the ditch, I had a sense of where we were. We were at the same point where I had been a few hours before.

"We're about forty feet from the top of the highwall," I announced.

Leah and Dr. C. C. both looked up the steep climb and moaned.

"The good news," said Leah, "is that it hasn't gotten any hotter since noon. The bad news is that it's still ninety-five degrees."

She helped Dr. C. C. sit down with his back against the steep slope. It wasn't easy. One wrong move and both of them would have rolled back into the trees. I braced myself with my heels dug into the hillside and removed my backpack so I could pass out some water.

"You children will go on without me," said Dr. C. C. "I cannot another step take."

"I was here just a few hours ago," I said. "We can take a lateral path to the west for about sixty yards, and we'll come out on the ridge."

"All this way I did not come that we should reveal ourselves to the villain," said Dr. C. C.

I had no answer to that.

Leah did.

"Dr. C. C.," she said, "we should get you to a place where you can rest."

"I will rest here," he said.

"You'll boil in this heat and humidity," Leah protested.

"I had to climb to the top straight up from here on my hands and knees," I said. "We should move to the ridge."

Dr. C. C. took his large right hand and mopped his soaking brow. For the first time I noticed he was not wearing his upside-down flowerpot.

"You are right, both of you," he said. "Let us get away from here."

24

RUMBLE

"So, you weren't able to get a cell signal from here?" Leah asked me.

I closed my eyes, let out a long breath, and dropped my head. *What an idiot I am*, I thought. When I had been up here after lunch, I should have checked for a signal before climbing straight up on my hands and knees. With my eyes closed and my head down, I waited for Leah to point out this obvious fact. She surprised me.

"Yeah, well," she said, "I guess there was no need for you to try and get a signal here. We were planning on looking down from the top of the highwall anyway."

We had decided that we should call Peggy and Calvin Branch and have them come pick us up on the ridge. There was no way we could go back down the way we had come up. And a trek from the ridge to where Dr. C. C. parked in that ditch would take forever—if we could even find it again. The Branches had a key to the gate that blocked the dirt road leading up to the fossil site, so they could rescue us from the heat and from what I was beginning to think was a plan more silly than an upside-down flower pot hat.

"I'm not getting a signal," said Leah. "Try yours."

"Nothing," I said. "Dr. C. C.?"

"Carrying my cellular telephone in my shirt pocket, I was," he said. "It fell out when I stumbled somewhere back there."

He waved a hand in the vicinity of the woods down the hill behind us.

"Lost my cellular telephone, I did, at the same time I lost my hat," he said. "I can get another cellular telephone. I will so miss that hat."

He seemed downright sad about his hat. I wanted to encourage him and say something like, *We can come back for your hat another time.* I knew better. If we ever got off the side of that hill, none of us would be back.

"Dr. Carroll," Leah said, "I'll buy you another hat."

"Yes, sir," I agreed. "I'll be happy to chip in for a new hat."

Dr. C. C. said, "Make them like that they do not anymore."

"Jason, let me have your phone," said Leah, "in case mine doesn't work up there."

"We have the same service," I said. I did not want to hand over my phone.

She didn't say anything—just reached out with her left hand.

"I'll go," I said.

Leah looked at me, and then with a slow turn of her head led me to follow her glance up the steep slope to where the top seemed to disappear into the sky.

"You already been up there once today. You sure you wanna climb it again?" she said.

I was sure I did not want to climb it again. I placed the phone in her outstretched hand.

"Thanks," I said.

A low rumble caused us all to turn toward the west. I remembered the lightning I had seen earlier. The strike that caused this new rumble had to be much closer.

"Ah, ha," said Dr. C. C. "It is about the time for our August afternoon thundershower."

"You say that as if it happens everyday," I said.

"August afternoon thunderstorms are something of a tradition in the south," said Leah.

"Indeed," said Dr. C. C. "There is, of course, about as good a chance it will miss us as there is it will hit us, but it is a chance we should not wish to take."

"Would be fun to watch from the highwall," I said.

"And dangerous," said Leah.

"Y'all wait here," she said. "I'll make the call, and when I come back down, we'll climb over to the ridge together."

She tightened her backpack on her shoulders, and took off up the hill.

25

Rabbits in the Sky

She was gone a long time.

Dr. C. C. didn't seem to notice. He made himself as comfortable as he could leaning back on his elbows against the steep hill. A billowy cloud covered us with its shadow and dropped the temperature a few degrees. It even brought with it a slight breeze.

"Still intensely hot," said Dr. C. C., "but the cloud gives us an illusion that maybe it will be cooling, does it not? It is an illusion we can hold onto. It reminds me of when I first met your father. That was before you were born, perhaps; I do not remember that he had a son when he and I first met. How hold are you now, Jason?"

"Fourteen," I answered.

"Yes," he said. "Before you were born I knew your father. Back then, and it was not seeming to be so long ago, our instruments were less precise than they are today. We had to be so very careful that the data we examined were not just an illusion created by instruments not up to the task."

I said, "My dad . . . I don't think I've ever heard him talk about illusions. I've heard him say things like, 'Are the data good?'"

"That is because he is an accomplished scientist, your father is," said Dr. C. C. "But your father is young. When he is older as am I, he can get away with asking, 'Are the data real, or is this but an illusion?'" He sat up enough to wave both hands in the air with his fingers fluttering as if conjuring a magic trick.

Funny. I never thought of my dad as young. I guess I never thought of him as old, either. He was just my dad. I'll admit it felt good to hear Dr. C. C. say my dad was an "accomplished" scientist.

"So how do you know when the data are good or bad or real or an illusion?" I asked.

"Ah, ha," he said, "is not that the question?"

He folded his hands behind his head and laid back to stare skyward.

"Look there," he said. He didn't have to point. I knew he was talking about the cloud. I laid back and stared into it.

"Do you see the rabbit?" he asked.

"No, sir," I replied. "I think I see the head of a bear."

"And yet they are both illusions," he said. "Imagine that you lived but a thousand years ago."

A thousand years? I thought. *I can't imagine living fifteen years ago.*

"A thousand years ago you worked your fields," he continued. "The tiny hairs on your arm lifted slightly as a gentle breeze drifted across your field carried upon the shadow of a cloud. Perhaps there was the slightest whiff of salt on that breeze, and you would know this has come from the sea. You would look heavenward. What would you see? A rabbit? A bear? The face of God?"

I was pretty sure he was not looking to me for an answer, so I kept quiet and listened.

"Your fields need nourishment that can come only from above, from the clouds. Yes, you know that the sun plays a role, and you pay homage to the sun as the most brilliant object of the heavens. But without the nourishment of the clouds, the sun would scorch your fields. Your instruments of meterology, if I may call them so, are your own senses: the cooling of a cloud's shadow against your skin, the scent of the sea on the breeze, the whisper of rustling leaves, and the images. Looking up, what do you see?"

This time I guessed he was expecting an answer, "The bear is gone," I said. "I think I see an eagle."

"You see an eagle, and yet you know there is no eagle," said Dr. C. C. "You know that because in recent history we have developed instruments that provide data that are so much better than the fuzzy images we detect with our naked eye."

He was right. With the naked eye you can see a man in the moon. With binoculars you can see craters on the moon. With a telescope you can see the moons of other planets.

I stole a glance at my watch. It was 3:30. *Leah should be back by now*, I thought.

I was about to say something about it when Dr. C. C. said, "It makes me wonder . . . We have such good instruments now . . . We gather good data . . . real data . . . But how much better will our instruments be in but ten years? Twenty years? A hundred years? How much better will our data become? How much more real? How many of the images that we hold true today will turn out to be rabbits in the clouds?"

Dr. C. C. closed his eyes and exhaled a long sigh.

I didn't want to interrupt whatever mood he was settling into, so I counted to thirty before I said, "I'm going up to check on Leah."

26

TOCK

I t was 4:10. Then it was 4:45. And there was nothing
in between.

Then it was five minutes after five.

At twenty minutes 'til six, I was able to see beyond the
watch hanging from my belt, and I could see that my feet
were pointed uphill. I remember thinking, *I've rolled down
a mountain before.*

Then it was six o'clock.

No pain, I said to myself, and I think I said it out loud.

I tried to sit up. I rose up on my elbows. It was too steep.
I didn't want to lie back down, so I scooted around to get
my feet lower than my head. The rocks beneath me wobbled
with an odd sound. *Horses*, it sounded like horses clomping
down a city street.

Then it was 6:15.

I know because I glanced at my watch when I sat up to
look down. It was about fifty yards to the bottom of the steep
slope where I was resting. *Fifty yards, that would be about
forty-five meters*, I thought. I was trying to get my brain
working. I twisted around to look back over my shoulder.
I could see up about one hundred yards to where the gray

rocks seemed to disappear into a gray sky. *One hundred yards would be about ninety meters.*

Who cares?

And then it was 6:35.

I was surrounded by gray. Gray rocks. A gray sky. There was even a gray smell. That smell, I realized, was me. My shirt was soaked with sweat. *I need a shower*, I said, and this time I know I said it out loud.

I sat up and rested my hands on my knees. I bent at the waist and let my head drop down which shifted my weight just enough to cause me to slide downhill a few feet. I leaned back and caught myself. The sound of horses on pavement rattled around me as the rocks wobbled. There was no other sound. There were no songbirds singing. There were no crows cackling. No wind. And no voices. There should be voices. Someone calling to me. Someone shouting to see if I was hurt.

Maybe they couldn't see me.

Leah! I shouted.

Leah, I'm down here!

I don't remember lying back down. I don't remember closing my eyes. I don't remember opening my eyes. I just remember being on my back and staring into a gray sky. The sky was close, like if I could stand, I could reach up and touch it. I sat up, tried to stand, flipped over, and rolled several feet down the slope.

This time there was pain. Most of the pain was in my knees and elbows. *Pain can be a good thing*, I thought. *It lets you know you're still alive.*

I eased myself up on my aching elbows and looked down

between my feet. The last time I rolled down a mountain a tree broke my fall. I looked down the steep slope. There was nothing between me and the fall to the bottom.

I glanced at my watch. It was 6:54—*a.m. or p.m.*, I wondered. It had to be p.m. If it were the morning, it would have been dark when I first looked at my watch at 4:10.

And that's when it hit me.

I have a concussion, I said aloud. I must have been knocked out when I first fell down this slope. I must have hit my head, no telling how many times, as I rolled down these wobbling gray rocks. I've never been knocked out before. I've never been unconscious.

They say if you've had a blow to the head, you're supposed to stay awake. I had to stay awake. Between 4:10 and 4:45, I must have passed out. And all those other gaps in time . . . I must have been out. Now it was after six. I had to stay awake.

Someone would come for me if I could stay awake.

If I could just stay awake.

My elbows were killing me. I wriggled my feet into the rocks and pressed my heels into what felt like solid ground so I could brace myself. Then I lifted up off my elbows and slid my butt down toward my feet. I sat up and wrapped my arms around my legs. There I was sitting in an upright fetal position and wondering, *Where am I?*

I was in a huge pile of rubble of some kind. Rocky rubble. Gray rocky rubble. The rubble was above me, below me, and stretched out in front of me. To my right was a high, sheer wall. The steep pile of rubble I was sitting in seemed like it might have been a part of that wall at some time in the past. Out in front of me, the gray rocks were laid out in what looked like huge furrows that could have been plowed by the Jolly Green Giant if he had been farming rocks.

Above the giant rock furrows, a rocky ridge ran from my left to right and seemed to disappear into the sheer wall. To my left, the ridge dropped into a line of scraggly trees beyond which I could see nothing.

I checked my watch again: 6:57. Three minutes had passed since I last looked at it. That sounded about right. That meant I had not passed out again.

Okay, Jason, I said aloud to myself, *You know where you are in time; where are you in space?*

Talking out loud to yourself might seem a little crazy. I didn't care. It was better to hear something, even my own voice, than the nothing that surrounded me. I might have thought I was trapped in a dream had it not been for the pain in my elbows and knees.

Where are you? I asked myself.

And for this I had no answer.

I closed my eyes, and the instant it was dark behind my eyelids, I flashed them open again. I could hear my own pulse pounding in my ears. I had to stay awake. Another look at the watch. 6:58. Good. I was not losing time again. Was I losing my mind?

Leah. Why had I called her name? The last time I saw her was back in April, wasn't it? And this is August . . .

How can you know that? I said aloud to myself and to the rocky rubble around me. *How can you know when it is and not know where it is?*

I thought about Leah, remembering the first time I saw

her standing on that wooden fishing pier in the longleaf forest. I had this strange feeling . . . I wanted to close my eyes and let that image of Leah on the pier carry me to . . .

Don't you dare close your eyes! I exclaimed to myself. The rocks did not appear to be listening.

Even with my eyes open, the imaginary image of Leah standing on the pier appeared to change. She turned toward me. She raised her left hand and waved to me. She was no longer standing on a pier in a forest; she was far away down a long corridor. She was looking right at me. She was at an airport, and I was walking toward her.

Bit by bit the events of the past couple of days revealed themselves to me. I knew I was at the Steven C. Minkin Paleozoic Footprint Site somewhere near Jasper, Alabama. I knew that I had arrived the day before and that Leah and her dad had met me at the airport. I knew that Carl Morris had escaped and was last seen in a swamp north of Andalusia. The night before, we stayed with Dr. Curtis Carroll—Dr. C. C. is what I called him. The last thing I could remember was the last thing I said to Dr. C. C.

"I'm going up to check on Leah," I had said to him.

That was the last thing I could remember. It was not the most important thing. The most important thing was something Leah's dad had said to me the night before.

"And, Jason," he said to me, "you look after my little girl."

27

A Weird Rhythm

It had to be Carl Morris.

I twisted around so that I could look back up toward the top of the highwall. It was about a hundred feet . . . a hundred feet. Just less than an hour before, I had thought it was a hundred yards. When my sense of time was knocked crazy, it must have taken my sense of space with it. Anyway, a hundred feet was a lot better than a hundred yards if I was going to climb back up.

And I was going to climb back up.

Twisting around sent a few rocks below me tumbling downhill. I braced myself on my right elbow and watched as they bounced and rolled all the way to the bottom. Yeah, there was pain in my elbow. I couldn't worry about that. I had to go up.

And, Jason, you look after my little girl.

Deputy Shirley Pickens' words kept running through my head again and again and again. He had said it as a kind of joke. I knew that. It didn't matter. His words had new meaning now that I didn't know where she was.

I twisted all the way around and started climbing up on my hands and knees. The hurt in my battered knees was balanced by bruises on the palms of my hands. The only thing I could figure was that I must have stuck my hands out to break my fall on the way down. I crawled up maybe thirty feet before I had to pause and take a break and rub my aching knees with my aching palms.

It was still hot. Hot. Hot. Hot. Too hot. The sun was up over the tree line. Clouds covered it, though. Good thing, or I would have fried and died right there on the southwest face of that slope. I glanced at my watch: 7:15. Alabama is on the easternmost side of the Central Time Zone. That means the sun rises and sets earlier than it does to the west. And in mid-summer Daylight Savings Time was still in effect, so I figured I would have another hour of good light—not to mention heat—before the sun faded fast. I continued my climb.

When I had jumped off that mountain in Huntsville back in June, it was because someone was shooting at me. Had someone been shooting at me this time? Had I jumped and bounced and rolled down through these gray rocks until I knocked myself out? Or had someone taken me and tossed me off the side of the highwall? I shuddered. If I had gone over the highwall instead of the rocky slope off to the side, I would not have survived to have this conversation with myself.

It had to be Carl Morris.

I didn't know how it could be. I just knew that it had to be. Somehow he must have found out that Leah had come to this fossil site. How? How could he have known that? Right then it didn't matter how. It mattered that I find Leah.

She had gone up to the top of the highwall to make a

phone call. It should have taken her about fifteen minutes—
twenty at the most. When she didn't return in about forty-five
minutes, I went up to find her. That's the last thing I could
remember before I woke up with a concussion.

It had to be Carl Morris.

Yeah, Carl Morris might be up there somewhere. So
what? If he was up there, I was sure he thought I was dead.
Besides, the last time I saw Leah, she was going up. If I was
going to look for her, I had to go up, too.

I was able to establish a weird rhythm to my climbing. I
could not reach out too far from my body without the risk
of slipping backwards, so I stuck my right hand up about
twelve inches and followed with my left knee coming up as
close as I could get it to my left hand. Then I would stick out
my left hand about twelve inches followed by bringing my
right knee to my right hand. Hand out, knee up, hand out,
knee up, hand out, knee up . . . a weird rhythm.

I needed to talk to Leah. I needed to tell her that she was
right. "The rocks seem to flow from the top of the highwall
and cascade down like some sorta waterfall made of rocks."
That's what she said that morning when she first looked out
across the site. A waterfall made of rocks. Yeah, and there I
was trying to climb back up against the falls. I had to. I had
to make the climb, find her, and tell her she was right.

Hand out, knee up, hand out, knee up . . . My rhythm
kept me from looking up to see what progress I was making.
I paused to check, surprised to see that I was within ten to
fifteen feet of the top.

Dr. Kayem needed to know he was right, too. Why didn't
we listen to him when he tried to tell us what a stupid idea

it was to try and catch a fossil thief? He was right. It was stupid. Who else could have done it, though? Leah was right about that, too. The cops were not going to sit up all night trying to protect a rock no matter how many fossil footprints it had on it.

And yeah, it crossed my mind that the fossil thief or thieves might be responsible for Leah's disappearance and for me being bounced and rolled down through the rocks. Having just spent much of the day with fossil people, though, I knew better. People who wear hats like that are not going to throw a fourteen-year-old kid from the top of a highwall.

It had to be Carl Morris.

And if I was right, I was maybe ten to fifteen feet from coming face to face with him.

28

Over the Top

Not a sound: that's what I heard as I contemplated climbing the last few feet to the top. One thing about that kind of heat: the animals don't like to be out and about. And there was no wind, which kind of surprised me because I remembered the slight breeze Dr. C. C. and I felt not long before I climbed up to look for Leah. No animals, no wind, no sound. And I did not want to break the silence with wobbling rocks as I approached the top.

I got as close as I could to the top without peeking over and listened.

Nothing.

I would have to poke my head up.

I closed my eyes and tried to remember what the flat area at the top of the highwall looked like. A wave of dizziness swept over me, and a wave of nausea passed through me. I had to open my eyes before I threw up. I took a slow breath in through my nose and let it out through my mouth. How I craved a bottle of water. I had left my backpack with Dr. C. C., because I thought I would be right back to where he was. I wondered if he was still there.

No time to let my mind wander wondering about things

I had no control over. I needed to visualize the top of the highwall. Afraid to close my eyes again, I stared out to the northwest. I remembered seeing that lighting strike on the northwest horizon earlier in the day. The horizon appeared much closer now. Everything appeared closer. The gray clouds were thick and low. What I did not know at the time was that the clouds were building up into a thunderhead. What I did know was that the low clouds were darkening the sky to the point that I might not have as much daylight left as I first thought.

Visualize, visualize, visualize, I told myself.

Okay, the highwall faces west. Right now I'm on the south end of that west face. On the north end is the steep, grassy slope I climbed to get to the top. Up top is a narrow, grassy plateau that runs the length of the highwall rim. Away from the rim to the east is a stand of scraggly trees.

I had not paid much attention to those trees earlier, even when I heard what sounded like a muffled laugh. Wish I had. What I thought I remembered is that they seemed thick, more like tall weeds than trees.

If Carl Morris was still around, that's where he would be. With dusk and clouds closing in, the thick, weedy trees would give him cover. When I poked my head up over the top, I would have no cover. On the other hand, when I poked my head up over the top, he might be standing right there waiting to kick me in the face and knock me back down the rocks.

I poked my head up over the top.

A quick look revealed that my visualization was correct. I dropped my head back down.

Now what?

Making it up as I went had carried me that far. If I was to go any farther, I would need a plan, and nothing I could come up with felt like a good plan. Everything I could think of involved me having to expose myself on the grassy plateau. If Carl Morris had thrown me down the rocky slope, if he had been shooting at me and I had jumped down the rocky slope . . . no matter how it happened, it would have been because I was exposed on the grassy plateau.

Maybe coming up hadn't been such a good idea in the first place.

I looked down. It was a long, long way to the bottom. And I was still convinced that Leah would be up, not down.

I decided I would poke my head up again for a quick look and then crouch down and make my way along the tree line to the north side where I could look and see if Dr. C. C. was still there. If so, I would join him, and we would make our way back to his car and go for help. That would be the best thing I could do for Leah.

If Dr. C. C. was gone, then I would try and figure out what to do next. It was the best I could come up with.

Oh, how I wished I had not let her take my cell phone.

29

Hello, Jason

I poked my head up over the top.

Carl Morris was looking straight down at me.

He had a gun in his left hand.

"Hello, Jason," he said.

He drew his right leg back as far as he could and kicked.

I jerked back and away.

His foot clipped my nose.

My nose was not enough to stop his momentum.

His feet came from under him, and he went out over the edge, landing on his back with a wallop in the rocks right next to me.

He groaned as he rolled toward me.

For an instant it seemed we would be stuck there face to face.

Then we began to slide.

I dug in as hard as I could with my heels and my hands.

Carl Morris tried to sit up and swing his gun around toward me.

He sat up, and he was gone.

The rocks beneath him gave way, and he cascaded down the waterfall made of rocks.

He bounced and rolled and bounced and rolled and bounced and rolled.

Somewhere about halfway down, I saw the gun fly from his hand.

Somewhere about ten or twenty feet from the bottom he came to an abrupt halt.

He did not move.

I did.

I scrambled up over the top and rolled onto the grassy plateau.

As soon as I could draw a breath, I jumped to my feet and yelled.

"Leah!"

"Leah!"

"Leah!"

No answer.

30

The Speed of Sound

"Leah!"
"Leah!"
"Leah!"

Still no answer.

Looking for any sign of her, I saw none. I decided I would walk along the tree line and call her name into the thick trees while making my way north so I could check for Dr. C. C.

One step and those waves of dizziness and nausea swept over me again. I fell straight down to my knees, which shot pain up both thighs. The pain converged at the base of my spine and ran up into my brain where it bloomed. I fell forward and caught myself with my hands so that I was on all fours. Blood dripped from my nose and landed with a splat on the back of my left hand. The urge to lie down and close my eyes was overwhelming, and the only thing that kept me from doing just that was the fear. The fear that if I closed my eyes I would never open them again. The fear that I would never see Leah again.

A sudden gust of wind rushed across the plateau carrying with it dust from who knows how many miles away. It came from the southwest. I was facing northeast, otherwise I'm sure the dust would have blinded me. About twenty yards away, right at the tree line, something stark white caught my eye as the wind carried it toward the thicket of trees.

Stark white, I thought, *does not appear in nature at a place like this.*

I got to my feet and half ran, half staggered to where it had gone into the trees. It was a piece of torn paper, and it had wedged among the low branches of a skinny pine. I picked it up and read "Cordova quadrangle." It was a piece of one of the topographical maps Dr. Kayem had given us. I reached into my back pocket. My map was still there, and it was whole.

The way the wind had swept across the plateau, I couldn't be sure where the piece of Leah's map had come from. The wind blew from the southwest, so I looked back in that direction just as a bolt of lighting filled the sky. I counted to twenty-six before a boom rattled me and everything around me. There was no horizon to the west anymore— just a black wall descending from heaven to earth. It was so foreign to me that it took a second or two for me to realize it was a wall of rain.

It was getting dark fast. The wall of rain was blotting out everything behind it to the west, and it was moving my way. There was another flash of lightning and another rattling boom. This time it took a twenty-three count for the thunder to reach me.

The wind came harder and more steady. I raised a hand to protect my eyes from the dust it brought, and started walking back down the tree line calling Leah's name.

About ten feet down the line, something crunched under my foot. It was my cell phone. Or at least what was left of it. It had been stomped into the ground. There were branches broken from the trees near the wrecked phone, and it looked like someone had shoved their way into the thicket of trees at that spot in the tree line.

A flash preceded a roar by seventeen seconds. The storm was gaining on me faster than I could think. The thick woods of too-close-together trees were already dark. If the black wall of rain got there before I found Leah . . .

No reason to think about that; there was nothing I could do about it. All I could do was try and follow the broken branches into the woods and hope.

Something stark white again caught my eye. Another piece of Leah's topo map fluttered against the bottom of a tree about ten yards ahead. I picked it up and looked around. There was another piece maybe fifteen or so yards through the thick trees. She was leaving me a paper trail.

A bizarre glow seemed to fill the woods, and before I could even think about counting, a blast shook my teeth. Light travels at 186,000 miles a second. Sound travels at about 768 miles an hour. When you hear it at the same time you see it, lightning is close. Too close.

Another piece of topo map lay fifteen feet ahead.

She's leaving me a map by leaving me her map, I thought. And I would have laughed at my own bad joke except nothing about this was funny.

The wind shoved its way through the tops of the trees. If it got down into the trees, the paper trail would blow off course. Fifteen or so feet ahead there was another piece. I knelt down to pick it up as the woods filled with light and a simultaneous blast that would have knocked me down if I hadn't already been kneeling.

For several seconds I could comprehend nothing other than that last blast. It was as if the thunder was running around in my brain looking for a way to get out. I squeezed both palms against my ears, and when I let go I was surprised to find I could still hear. The problem was that what I heard did not sound all that great: cracking wood as the wind forced itself upon the scraggly trees that were no match for its power. And then, swirling around among the chaos that swirled around me, I heard the sweetest sound ever.

I heard my own name.

31

To the Light

There it was again, "Jason."

It was faint. Not faint like far away. Faint like weak. Like it was muffled.

Again, "Jason."

It whirled around in the wind. She had to be close. She must have seen me when that last blast of lightning illuminated the woods. How else would she have known I was there?

The first tiny ball of ice hit me on the side of the head above the right ear. An advance scout for much larger balls of hail, I suspected, that were moving ahead of the rain.

"Jason," swirled through the trees one more time.

I almost hoped for another bolt of lightning to light up the woods so I could see—almost.

I didn't dare move until I could figure out which direction to take. As faint as her voice was, I could have walked away a few feet in the wrong direction and never heard her again. Standing as still as I could in the buffeting wind, I listened.

"Men."

"Men."

"Men."

Maybe getting hit in the head knocked me crazy, I thought.

"Men."

"Men."

The words swept through again followed by what sounded like a gagging cough. Maybe it wasn't *men,* maybe it was . . .

I turned and faced the way I had been facing when the last bolt of lightning illuminated the woods. I imagined that direction as twelve o'clock. Then I turned to face ten o'clock. I walked about twenty yards, and there she was.

She was tied to a tree, her hands behind her back.

Darkness was swarming in on us fast. I felt where her hands were bound together. There was a knot in some kind of cloth. Before I could begin to try and untie it, Leah mumbled something incomprehensible.

I realize she had something in her mouth. I came around to face her, held her jaw with my left hand, and with my right pulled out what felt like a wad of paper.

"Stand back," she said.

And then she began to cough and spit.

"My red scarf," she said. "That's what he tied my hands with. Can you cut it?"

"My Swiss Army Knife is in my backpack," I said. "Don't know where the backpack is."

"Untie me, then, and hurry. Carl Morris is up here somewhere, and he has a gun."

"No," I said. "He lost the gun when he went bouncing down the rock cascade."

"You killed him?" she said.

It felt like somebody punched me in the stomach.

Was he dead?

There was no way for me to know.

As much as I hated the guy, it never occurred to me that I might have watched him die.

"Jason! Jason!" Leah snapped me out of my haze. "Please! Untie me!"

It wasn't easy. She had been trapped there for a long time. The scarf was soaked with sweat, which had tightened the knot.

"Hurry," she said, "You can hear the hail at the edge of the trees. It'll be here any second."

I dropped to my knees and gnawed at the knot with my teeth. One, two, three, and then a million little balls of ice pummeled us both.

When the knot broke loose, Leah yelled, "Get down!"

Even though I couldn't see or hear, I knew she had dropped straight forward from the tree. I crawled to her and covered her body with my own.

The hail didn't last long, which you might think was a good thing, except it was followed by a torrent of raindrops bigger than any I knew existed. The rain came in at us sideways, propelled, according to Leah, by a tornado. Trees and thunder cracked all around us as just overhead a freight train roared past.

The storm must have been waiting to catch that train, because as it rumbled to the northeast it took the wind and the rain with it. Leah and I uncurled from the ground we'd been trying to dig ourselves into and sat up.

"You look terrible," she said.

"Yeah, well, your hair's a mess," I replied.

Getting to my feet wasn't easy, and judging from the way Leah struggled, it was tough for her, too.

Through the scraggly trees, shafts of golden light beckoned us. We followed it through the woods and out toward the rim of the highwall. Far on the horizon the sun was a vivid, amber ball.

"Looks like the dawn of a new day," Leah said.

"Except that we're looking to the west, and the sun rises to the east," I said.

"You know what, Caldwell?" she said, "Sometimes you an' your book learnin' take the romance right outta things."

I was not sure I knew what she meant by that, so I kept my mouth shut.

32

First Things First

"We should find Dr. C. C.," I said.

"First things first," said Leah.

She walked over to the edge of the rim and peered down to her left.

"He's not moving," she said. "Wanna see?"

"I'll take your word for it," I said.

There was that punched in the stomach sensation again followed by a sick feeling.

"Maybe he'll be all right," I mumbled.

Leah didn't say anything. She turned and stared at me for a minute, then she walked up to me, put her arms around me, and hugged.

"You saved my life," she said.

"Does that mean we're even?" I said.

She let go of her hug and leaned back, placing both hands on my shoulders. She looked me straight in the eye and said, "We'll never be even."

With that she released me, and we started hobbling our way to the north end of the highwall. We were almost to the point where we would have to slide down that steep, forty foot hill when we saw the lights: flashing blue with a splash of yellow mixed in. There was a police car coming up over the ridge. Leah and I walked as close to the edge of the highwall as possible in the hope they would see us. The car came to a halt at the point along the ridge where the canopies had been set up earlier in the day. I could see the blue tarp covering the trackways we were supposed to be guarding.

"Children! Children!"

A voice was calling from the bullhorn atop the police car. It sounded familiar. It sounded like "Chill-ren! Chill-ren!"

"Remind me to find out where he's from," I said. "I've been trying to guess that accent . . ."

"New Orleans," said Leah. "He's from New Orleans, but that doesn't totally explain the accent. His father was Nigerian and his mother French-Canadian. So he grew up speaking English with French influences from three different parts of the world."

"I would be impressed if I wasn't in such pain," I said.

We waved at the car. The flashing lights went off, and the high beams blinked, which we took as an indication they saw us. Two officers stepped from the front of the car and Dr. C. C. from the back. They all waved in our direction. We hobbled onward toward the slope. One of the officers walked in a direction that would intersect with us.

We got to the steep, forty-foot slope and slid down on our rear ends. My backpack was not there, washed away, I supposed, by the torrential rains.

"A granola bar and a bottle of water sure would be good," said Leah.

All of the joints I banged up when I fell down that rocky

cascade began to pulse in pain at once. Leah struggled to her feet so she could make the last leg of the journey around to the ridge.

"Hold on a second," I said.

She turned to face me.

"You need a hand?" she asked.

"I need to know how he found us," I replied.

She sat back down and breathed a big sigh. She had to be in a lot of pain, too. She had been tied to that tree with her hands behind her back for who-knows-how-long. And all she could do was stand there that whole time.

"You okay?" I said.

She nodded and drew another breath. She laid back against the hill much like Dr. C. C. had when he was spotting rabbits in the sky.

"So, how did Carl Morris know where to find us?" I said. "And don't tell me he just happened to be hiding in this area. There's no way this was a coincidence."

"The *Andalusia Star News* has a section they call "Neighbors," said Leah. "They print little tidbits about people around the community. Apparently there was a tidbit about the daughter of Deputy Shirley Pickens visiting the Steven C. Minkin Paleozoic Footprint Site."

I almost said, *You told the newspaper?* I'm glad I didn't.

Leah said, "When I find out who told the newspaper, I'm going to kick their butt."

"Call me," I said. "I'd like to help."

"Yeah," said Leah. "Morris was braggin' he had folks in Andalusia who saw it in the paper. Said he had folks lookin' out for him. I told him I was surprised he knew anyone who could read. That's when he stuck that wad of paper in my mouth."

The shadows of trees just below us were getting longer to the east with every passing second.

"It's gonna be dark real soon," Leah said.

She stood and offered a hand to help me up. I needed all the help I could get. She pulled me up and took off ahead of me. I tried not to make too many grunts and groans as we made our way around to the ridge.

I said, "So that's how he knew we were here . . . wait a minute. Was I in the paper, too?"

"No," she said.

"How did he . . . yeah, well, I guess he came looking for you and found me at the same time."

"Something like that," she agreed.

"That doesn't explain how he knew we would be up on the highwall," I said.

"You told him," said Leah.

She stopped and turned toward me with dramatic flair. If her hair hadn't been matted down with rain and sweat, I'm sure it would have done that thing where it seems to swirl around her face in slow motion like in a shampoo commercial. She was between me and the setting sun, so all I could see was her silhouette framed in a golden hue.

"He was up there looking down on us when you went up to test for cell phone coverage," she said. "When he saw you coming up, he hid in the trees and heard you on the phone telling somebody we would be up there this evening."

"My little sister," I said. "I told Phoebe to tell my mom and dad."

"Yeah," Leah continued, "he told me all about it when he had me tied to that tree. How he wasn't as dumb as I thought he was. How he was gonna throw my little science boy . . ."

"Science boy?" I said.

"That's what he called you. Science boy. Only he called you *my* little science boy. Like I had my own personal little science boy. Sorta cute, don't ya think?"

"Not at all," I said.

"Whatever," she said. "He was gonna throw you off the top of the mountain, as he called it. I tried to tell the idiot that it wasn't a mountain, but it just seemed to make him mad."

"Why me?" I said. "Why would he throw me and not you?"

"For one thing, I never jabbed him in the face with an axe," said Leah. "Or maybe he don't like science. Or little science boys."

I grunted, and started walking on toward the ridge.

"Let's go," I said.

Leah blocked my path and said, "He had the bright idea he could use me to get at my daddy. My daddy's put four Morrises in jail already. Ain't but a couple of them left. And when they find out who told Carl about that newspaper article, I imagine there'll be one more of 'em in jail."

She turned and continued toward the ridge. I hobbled as fast as I could to keep up. Without looking back she said, "Well, Caldwell, it looks like you finally made it to Alabama without someone shooting at you."

33

CRUMPLED

A Walker County deputy sheriff reached out and offered Leah a hand as we made the last few steps taking us away from the highwall and onto the ridge.

"Leah Pickens?" asked the deputy.

"Yes, sir," Leah replied.

The deputy spoke into a microphone clipped to the top of his left shoulder. "We've got her," he said.

"Your dad called," said the deputy. "Something about a newspaper article and an escaped convict. Not sure of the details, but we got out here soon as we could after the weather blew through. Found your professor walking along Old Kirkpatrick Road."

When the deputy was sure that Leah had sound footing on the ridge, he turned to me. One look and he spoke again into his microphone.

"We need an ambulance," he said.

Something about the idea that we were going to be safe gave my body permission to go into hyperpain. I tried to step toward the deputy and couldn't move. He reached out and grabbed me when I started weaving like tall grass in a slow wind.

"Hang on," he said.

He and Leah helped walk me out onto the ridge. We paused, and the deputy stood back to look me over.

"Can you make it to the car, or do you need to rest here?" he asked me.

I answered, "I'll make it . . . with help."

Leah said, "That escaped convict? He's crumbled up on the south end of the highwall."

"Crumpled," I said.

"What?" said Leah.

"What?" said the deputy.

I said, "He's not crumbled. He's crumpled. Cookies crumble. People crumple."

"Caldwell," said Leah, "I can't believe you. But one more crack like that and me an' this deputy are gonna leave you crumpled up here among these crumbled rocks."

I felt it best not to mention that she should have said, *The deputy and I.*

The deputy said something about a crumpled or crumbled convict in the crumpled or crumbled rocks and I saw the deputy back at the police car open the trunk.

Dr. C. C. met us about halfway to the car.

"Children, it is gone," were the first words he said to us.

Leah and I didn't have to ask. We knew he was talking about the Oneonta girls' slab of trackways.

At the time, Dr. C. C. knew nothing about Carl Morris. He didn't know about Leah being tied to a tree. He didn't know about me being tossed over the side of the highwall. And neither of us had the energy to explain.

When we got to the blue tarp that was supposed to be covering the slab, Dr. C. C. lifted it to show us. A single pink peanut drifted out from under the tarp and floated across the fossil site.

"Gone," he said. "Gone."

I tried not to appear too happy to see my backpack under the tarp. I didn't want him to think I wasn't unhappy about the loss of the slab.

"Water," I said.

"Water," said Leah.

She took my backpack out from under the tarp and brushed a couple of pink peanuts from it. Then she opened it and pulled out two beautiful bottles of water.

The deputy with the binoculars said, "There he is."

He had his binoculars trained on the cascade of rocks.

"He ain't movin'," he said.

The first deputy helped me to the front of the car where I leaned against the hood. The second deputy handed him the binoculars, then reached into the car and unfastened a shotgun.

"Not moving. Is he dead?" said the first as he looked through the binoculars.

"Think so," said Leah.

"Maybe not," I said.

"You go," said the first deputy. "I'll stay with the kids."

The second deputy said, "Is he armed?"

"Lost his gun," I said. "I saw him lose it as he fell."

Deputy number two made sure his shotgun was loaded

and started toward the cascade of rocks where Carl Morris lay.

Deputy number one spoke into his microphone. He said something about a Life Saver helicopter. For me he called an ambulance. For Carl Morris he called a helicopter.

Dr. C. C. still wasn't sure what was going on.

"When you did not return right away," said Dr. C. C., "I made my way to the ridge with your backpack. I knew I could follow the road out of here and find help. But the storm came upon me so fast, I covered myself with the tarp to wait it out. And, of course, I discovered we had been robbed. I have told these fine officers about the theft."

The fine officers were unconcerned about the loss of fossil trackways.

They *were* concerned about the crumpled Carl Morris.

As we waited for an ambulance and a helicopter, Leah and I told the first deputy all about it. And as a bonus for Dr. C. C., we told him who stole the trackways.

34

PEANUTS

I spent the night in the same hospital as Carl Morris. He was in the trauma unit. I was in a room somewhere on one of the upper floors. Having been in the hospital after rolling down a mountain just a couple of months before, I knew the drill. Doctors came in every hour on the hour and poked and probed me to make sure I could still feel pain—that I was still alive.

This hospital was at UAB—the University of Alabama at Birmingham—and it's a teaching hospital. The doctors traveled with a flock of student doctors all in white lab coats. After the main doctor jabbed me a few times and flashed lights in my eyes, one or two of the students would do the same thing. Then they would talk about me as if I couldn't hear them standing right next to me. They seemed concerned that I couldn't remember being thrown off the highwall and about my lapses in time during the couple hours I spent lying among the rocks. When they were finished, the main doc would say something like, "No big deal. It's not unusual to forget a traumatic event like being hurled from a great height. You'll be fine."

You'll be fine. Right. Tell that to my knees and elbows.

I'll admit, I felt a little better when I found out Carl Morris was not dead. At least that's what I thought until two U.S. marshals walked into my room.

"Carl Morris says you tried to kill him," said the first marshal.

"With my nose," I said.

There was a big, white bandage on my nose where he had kicked me. I tried not to look at it, afraid I might go cross-eyed.

The marshal opened a yellow legal pad to a clean page and pulled a pen from his pocket.

"Yes," he said. "Your girlfriend told us what happened. We need to see how your story matches with hers."

I doubted it would do any good to tell them she was not my girlfriend, so I just told them what had happened.

"Do our stories match?" I said after about thirty minutes of telling the tale.

The marshal stuck his pen back in his pocket and said, "Very much so."

He and his fellow marshal both said something to the effect of, "Get well soon," and left.

Deputy Shirley Pickens and two other deputies walked into the room as they were leaving.

"Jason," said Deputy Pickens, "how you doing?"

"I would be better," I said, "if I could take a shower. At least with this bandage on my nose I can't smell myself."

Deputy Pickens introduced me to Deputy Sandra Hayes from Covington County and Deputy Bill Walker from Walker County. Walker from Walker was the same deputy who first met Leah and me coming down from the highwall.

"The deputies want to ask you some questions," said Deputy Pickens. "I'm going to step out because my daughter was involved, and we don't want to give the impression that there was any influence on your testimony."

"Testimony?" I said. "Sounds so legal."

"Crimes were committed," said Deputy Hayes.

Deputy Pickens left, and I spent another thirty minutes retelling the same story I'd just told the marshals. I even threw in the bit about trying to kill Carl Morris with my nose. They were not amused.

They left, and in came Leah and a man from the ABI, the Alabama Bureau of Investigation. I was about to suggest he call anybody else who might want to hear the tale so I wouldn't have to keep repeating myself.

Leah said, "Agent Arnold is here about the trackways."

"The State of Alabama controls the Steven C. Minkin Paleozoic Footprint Site," said Agent Arnold. "We found the slab in the back of Calvin Branch's SUV after the Walker County Sheriff's Office called us. Just wanted to confirm how you and your girlfriend knew it was him."

"First of all, the whole stupid plan was his idea," I said. "And he made sure he would be the last one to leave the site before we had a chance to get to the top of the highwall. It was his idea to cover the slab with a tarp. That way, when we watched from the highwall, we would see the tarp and have no way of knowing the fossils were not under it. It was a good plan: setting himself up as the hero when he was the real thief."

"Caldwell," said Leah, "I can't believe you."

"What?" I said.

Agent Arnold turned toward Leah with a wrinkled brow.

"You never woulda known if you hadn't seen those pink peanuts," she said.

Agent Arnold tried to say something about Styrofoam peanuts when Leah cut him off.

"Don't let my little science boy fool you," she said. "He's sorta smart, but he ain't nearly as smart as he tries to let on."

"Hey," I said, "Those pink peanuts could have come from anywhere."

"They came from Branch's SUV, an' you know it," Leah insisted.

"I know it now," I said. "You add up all the evidence and the peanuts confirm it."

"Branch musta had peanuts stuck on him when he got up under that tarp to grab the slab," Leah said.

"Right," I said. "And the peanuts confirmed my suspicions."

"Confirmed your suspicions," Leah mocked me. "You didn't have no suspicions 'til you saw those peanuts."

"Regardless," said Agent Arnold. "It was Calvin Branch who has been stealing and selling fossils. We don't believe his wife knew anything about it."

He said goodbye and turned to leave when Leah grabbed his arm and stopped him.

"Agent Arnold," she said, "one more thing you need to know for your investigation."

The agent wrinkled his brow again.

"I ain't his girlfriend."

35

GRITS

Leah and her dad spent the rest of the night dozing in the uncomfortable chairs in my hospital room. I was glad. My mom and dad couldn't get a flight to Birmingham until the next morning. Trying to sleep proved impossible for me. I was still afraid to close my eyes. Still afraid I might start losing time again.

At 6 A.M. a new flock of doctors came in and verified that I was still in a lot of pain. A few minutes later an orderly entered with what I assumed was breakfast. Deputy Pickens mumbled something about coffee and left the room. Leah stood up from her chair and stretched. She bent at the waist and shook her hair for a minute or two.

When she stood back upright, she said, "I need a shower. And judging from the aroma in this room, so do you."

"Not me," I said. "It's the breakfast."

She laughed. Her dark eyes seemed to fill with light. She stepped toward me and snatched the biscuit from my plate. "Well, if you ain't gonna eat it," she said.

That same weird feeling I had in my stomach when I was walking down the concourse to meet her at the Birmingham airport swept through me.

"You not hungry?" she said.

"Yeah, I should eat," I said.

There was a pile of some odd white substance sitting next to the scrambled eggs on my plate. I pointed to it and said, "What's that?"

"You never had grits before?" Leah seemed shocked.

"I've got grit under my fingernails," I said. "Try not to eat it."

"Not grit, *grits*," she said. "This is your third trip to Alabama, and you've had no grits?"

I felt like I was being accused of breaking an Alabama law.

"Well," I said, "The first time we were here we camped, and we cooked our own food. The second time we stayed in a cabin at a state park, and we cooked our own food. The Caldwells don't travel with a grit."

"Not grit," Leah repeated, "*grits*."

She unwrapped a little pat of butter and put it on the grit—or grits. Then she opened the little pepper packet and sprinkled some on it or them. She scooped a bit onto a spoon and placed it to my lips. I closed my eyes and took a small bite. The grits were warm and soft, and for that single instant they were the best thing I had ever tasted in my life.

When I opened my eyes the spoon was stuck in the grits.

"Good, huh?" said Leah.

"Good," I agreed.

ABOUT THE AUTHOR

Roger Reid is an Emmy Award-winning writer, director, and producer for the *Discovering Alabama* television series, a program of the University of Alabama's Alabama Museum of Natural History in cooperation with Alabama Public Television. He is the author of two other young adult novels starring Jason Caldwell, *Longleaf* and *Space*, both published by NewSouth Books. He lives with his family in Birmingham.

To learn more about *Time*
and get news of Jason's further adventures,
visit **www.rogerreidbooks.com**
and **www.newsouthbooks.com/time**